SURVIVOR'S REVENGE

Walter Keith

Published by Walter Keith, 2024.

This is a work of fiction. Similarities to real people, places, or events are entirely coincidental.

SURVIVOR'S REVENGE

First edition. July 31, 2024.

ISBN: 979-8227114624

Written by Walter Keith.

To my wife Anita who has put up with me all these years

PROLOGUE

In 2090, Earth is the target of a brutal attack by the Roton Empire's alien Starship, leaving the planet devoid of human life. In response, the Galuten Empire, a society led by resilient women, sends its powerful hunter-killer starship to confront the alien invaders and restore order to the universe. Amidst the chaos and destruction, one lone survivor emerges - John Pope, a former Master Sergeant in the United States Army Special Forces. With his experience facing adversity and danger, Pope must now face new challenges that will push him to his limits and test his courage and determination like never before. Joining the Galuten Empire's Starship 36, Pope embarks on a remarkable journey of bravery, selflessness, and redemption as he navigates the perils of intergalactic warfare. Along the way, he forges unexpected alliances, battles formidable enemies, and discovers an inner strength he never knew existed - all leading to his ultimate goal: revenge on the Rotons for their devastating attack on Earth.

As John Pope rises through the ranks to become a laser fire control officer in the Galactic Empire's Space Fleet, his ultimate goal becomes clear - to seek revenge for the senseless destruction of his world and its people by the cruel Roton Empire. With all of his being, the Pope is determined to bring justice to those who have caused him and his people such harm. But in his quest for vengeance, he must contend with enemies on the outside and the turmoil in his heart. As Pope walks the line between hero and villain, Pope grapples with his mission's moral complexities and the toll it takes on his soul. In battle, he must confront his inner demons and find the courage to forge a new destiny. With determination burning in his heart, John Pope embarks on an epic journey across the galaxy to seek revenge against the Rotons who destroyed Earth.

Chapter 1

Our mission, a brief interlude from the relentless chaos of the battlefield, gave us a much-needed respite. Here, we found a moment of peace. It was a necessary break from the constant noise and destruction surrounding us, a chance to recharge before returning to the front lines. Despite the violence and turmoil of war, this slight reprieve gave us hope for a better, calmer tomorrow. As I glance around at my comrades, I witness them seizing this rare opportunity to unwind and rejuvenate, their expressions bearing the physical and mental exhaustion of unrelenting combat. Master Sergeant John Pope stands tall, his posture exuding strength and authority. He has a chiseled, weather-worn face that reflects years of military service. His uniform is crisp and perfectly pressed. His team includes Sergeant Fred Mayer, Sergeant Mary Barlow, and Corporal Bill O'Connor, each bringing their unique expertise to create a cohesive unit. Our mission is simple yet essential: to inventory and inspect small arms, ensuring their certification for use in the field. Our duty as guardians goes beyond self-preservation; we provide the reliability and effectiveness of weaponry for our comrades on the front lines. By doing so, we contribute significantly to the security of our nation.

I distributed tasks among my team, assigning each member specific daily responsibilities. "Sergeant Clark, please conduct an inventory check on the M35 rifles and ensure they are in top condition." "Sergeant Meyer, you will be responsible for documenting the new ammunition designed for the M35 rifles." "Corporal O'Connor, please complete an inventory of the new 9-millimeter handguns and their accompanying ammunition." "We must be completed by noon." After lunch, We will regroup in the Post Training Room to receive testing procedure updates. Everyone must attend and pay attention." I turned to Sergeant Clark and requested more information about the new M35 rifles. "These rifles have advanced fire control technology, including target tracking and heads-up displays. These advancements greatly improve accuracy and reduce human error, even at long distances." I emphasized the importance of ensuring the rifles are in top shape for field testing. During a conversation with Sergeant Meyer, I learned about a fascinating feature of the 9-millimeter handguns. Each comes with a unique wristwatch that acts as a micro transmitter, preventing unauthorized individuals from firing the weapon. I expressed my admiration for this impressive technology. Continuing our discussion, I asked about the progress of counting the M35 magazines. Sergeant Meyer confirmed that he had completed the inventory check but noticed that the manufacturer marked each bullet uniquely. He was Intrigued by this observation, so I asked him to explain further. He replied, "These rounds maintain near-pinpoint accuracy even when fired by inexperienced shooters and at long distances." This remarkable feature left him impressed yet slightly unnerved.

As we put the finishing touches on our assignments, the air suddenly filled with blaring alarms and flashing lights. The steel door slammed shut, blocking out all noise from the outside world. Our bunker's backup generator kicked in, providing a reliable power source. We could feel the Class 10,000 HEPA filtration system humming to life, ensuring that the air in our shelter remained clean and safe. At first, I thought there had been a malfunction in the security system that had caused this sudden lockdown. I frantically tried to contact the command post for help, but my calls went unanswered. The feeling of isolation and uncertainty only increased.

Determined to gather information, I turned on the bunker camera system. With a mixture of apprehension and curiosity, I activated the cameras and saw a horrifying sight: lifeless bodies scattered outside our shelter. It made no sense why anyone would target us here - we were of no strategic importance. Realizing that we were trapped until the system reset, I searched the bunker manual for a way to override the lockdown. But it became clear that our only option was to wait patiently for the system to clear and allow us to investigate the unfolding events outside. As time passed, a sense of urgency began to build among our group. We knew we had to prepare for whatever lay beyond the blast door. Pope's voice echoed through the dimly lit bunker as he addressed the team, their heavy boots clattering on the concrete floor. He handed out M35 rifles, making sure each man had enough ammunition—the corporal aimed to obtain a grenade launcher and gather ample grenades.

We all knew the plan - wait for the all-clear, then rush out the blast door. I reminded the team I would lead the way, ducking behind cover until I reached the Hummer parked just outside.

After an eternity, we finally received a clear and unmistakable signal. Cautiously, we waited as the blast door slowly opened, revealing the outside world hidden from us for so long. Stepping out of the bunkerThe eerie stillness pressed down on me as I surveyed the scene. My heart thudded in my chest as my gaze landed on Lieutenant Baker's motionless form sprawled out on the ground. His usually vibrant face was now pale and lifeless, his eyes staring blankly at the sky. The silence was deafening. It was a chilling sight, made all the more puzzling by the lack of visible injuries. Suspicions pointed towards his death caused by lethal gas, as there were no other plausible explanations.

What puzzled me even more was that this gas seemed to spare the lives of two deer peacefully grazing nearby. The source and motive behind this attack remained a mystery, leaving countless questions that demanded immediate attention and investigation. Gathering the rest of our team, we examined the other deceased personnel at the base, only to find that they appeared to have died in the same manner. Desperate for answers, we went to the base's command post, hoping to establish communication with the outside world. However, all attempts to contact the command center or access the Internet proved futile, suggesting that this devastating event may have affected the entire globe. Driven by our need for information, we ventured into nearby communities. Before leaving, we moved the deceased into an empty building to protect them from wild animals.

We boarded a Hummer and began our journey, only to be greeted by a disturbing sight: an enormous ship hovering ominously three miles away at the uranium mining site. To our surprise, a smaller vessel was released from the ship and made its way to the mining site. We estimated it would take about three miles to reach the site where we saw it land. When we were about half a mile away, we stopped the Hummer and continued on foot through dense vegetation and forest to avoid being spotted by anyone at the landing site.

As we approached the landing site, our boots sinking into the soft soil, a strange sight greeted us. Six towering beings stood before us, their slender limbs encased in a shimmering pink shell that seemed to pulse with energy. Their insectoid heads swiveled towards us, their four unsettling eyes fixated on our every move. Four creatures were busy setting up intricate equipment, while the remaining two stood guard with weapons at the ready.

Without warning, Barlow sprang into action, her M35 weapon held firmly in her hands. She fired at the aliens, but her shots merely ricocheted off their impenetrable armor. The creatures turned and hissed in anger, undeterred by her futile attempt. Mayer adjusted her aim, determined to take them down no matter what it took. She zeroed in on one of the four-eyed heads of the aliens, watching as her precise shot caused it to explode in a burst of vibrant purple liquid. The remaining aliens retaliated with a barrage of energy and laser weapons, striking Barlow and causing her body to fall lifelessly to the ground. In the chaos, Sergeant Clark and Corporal O'Connor bravely threw grenades at the enemy's landing craft, causing it to topple and explodeTheir brave and selfless act, while bold, did not come without a cost. Struck down by a barrage of enemy fire, their bodies fell limp and lifeless on the battlefield. Those who witnessed their heroism will forever remember and honor their sacrifices. I frantically fired my weapon at two more approaching aliens, barely able to hear the sound of gunfire from Sergeant Clark's rifle before he also met his demise. Seeking cover behind a nearby brick wall, I had no time to mourn as I continued my fierce fight against the overwhelming odds. With determination fueling my every move, I refused to give up even as my heart raced and my breaths became shallow. Only two aliens remained, their bug-like heads swiveling as they prepared for their next attack. But I was ready, determined to take down as many as possible before my inevitable end.

A loud explosion shattered the air around me. Simultaneously, another spacecraft unleashed a barrage of missiles at the unknown vessel, causing it to burst into flames and sending shards of shrapnel flying in every direction. I had no clue what was transpiring above my head.

IN A HIGH-STAKES ENCOUNTER, Starship 136 of the Galuten Empire relentlessly chased an enemy vessel from the Roten Empire. Their pursuit led them to track the distinct trail the ship's powerful engines left behind as it traveled through the Wormhole. The Galutens believed this vessel could be one of the infamous planet killers, a devastating weapon used by their enemies. The two empires are engaged in a century-long conflict sparked by Roten attacks on two of Galuten's planets using DNA-directed gas. However, the Galutens were able to push back the Rotens and regain control of their territory, with their vigilant Space Force constantly monitoring for any incursions. Within the fleet, Starship 136 was renowned for its advanced technology and success in neutralizing several Roten vessels, proving its capabilities time after time.

The Galuten empire experienced a monumental revelation centuries ago when they discovered the Wormholes, previously explored by an ancient civilization that had long disappeared. It is believed that this advanced race mapped out the Wormholes and shaped numerous star systems that now hold intelligent lifeforms.

EMERGING FROM THE WORMHOLE, the Galuten Heavy Cruiser set a course towards the third planet to engage an enemy vessel. The journey would take approximately forty-eight hours, giving the crew time to prepare for the upcoming battle. Utilizing stealth mode by the cruiser aimed to avoid detection by the enemy's advanced sensors and maintain the element of surprise. Under Empire command, Starship 136 had diligently tracked the enemy ship through its ion trail within the Wormhole. This enemy vessel was known as a planet killer, dispatched by the ruthless Roton Empire, notorious for their brutal tactics and relentless pursuit of conquest. A long-standing conflict between the Goliten and Roton Empires stemmed from the Roton's use of human DNA gas on Goliten planets in an attempt to conquer and colonize them under their insect queen rulers. Despite facing many challenges, the Galutens successfully repelled the Rotons from their territory with the help of constant monitoring and intervention by their Space Force. Starship 136, a state-of-the-art vessel in their fleet, was explicitly designed for pursuing and engaging hostile adversaries. As they approached the end of the Wormhole, the ion trail intensified, signaling their imminent emergence into unknown territory. Captain

Chrona immediately ordered her crew to prepare for combat while gathering available intelligence on the planetary system ahead. "Commander, do we have any information on this habitable planet in our database?" Captain Chrona asked sternly. "Yes, Captain. I have the report right here," replied Commander Larrson. "Excellent, give it to me," Captain Chrona eagerly took the report from her second-in-command.

THE LATEST REPORT FROM Survey Starship 120, STS 34-1274, confirms the successful mapping of Wormhole 45. Exiting the Wormhole, our team discovered a star system with eight planets. Further exploration revealed signs of intelligent life on the third planet from its sun, which we now know is called Earth. However, Earth seems to be in a state of conflict, as our sensors detected an atomic blast between nations. We advise against contacting them at this time due to their violent situation. We did capture radio communications from the planet in various languages for future reference.

EMERGING SWIFTLY FROM the Wormhole, the Galuten Heavy Cruiser immediately set its course towards the third planet to intercept the enemy's ship. It would reach the optimal firing distance in approximately twenty-eight hours and activate its stealth mode, rendering it invisible to the enemy's advanced detection systems. The commander, fully aware of the gravity of the situation, promptly ordered Lieutenant Sar to load two size-five missiles into the firing bays per the Captain's specific instructions. Seeking assurance of the missiles' effectiveness, the commander turned to Lieutenant Sar, who confidently confirmed that the Captain had requested them. With a sense of urgency, the commander instructed, "Lieutenant Sar, oversee the loading process of these missiles into firing bays one and two." As these missiles had been in storage for some time, Lieutenant Sar must also conduct thorough diagnostics to ensure their optimal functionality. Satisfied with the instructions, the commander quickly returned to the bridge and awaited confirmation of successful loading from Lieutenant Sar. Moments later, she reported back that all rockets were ready to fire.

The Lieutenant's eyes flickered with determination as she gripped the control panel and gave a curt nod to the Captain. "We're approaching the Roton's ship now, sir. We'll be within range in less than an hour." As we closed in on our target, the Lieutenant watched the countdown timer intensely until it read 00:00. With her finger hovering over the launch button, she awaited the Captain's command. "Lieutenant," she said, her voice steady and commanding. "We are now within range. You may begin firing at your discretion." Without hesitation, she pressed the button twice, unleashing two missiles that struck the Roton's ship with deadly precision. Explosions bloomed across its surface, tearing it apart into unrecognizable pieces. Our sensors scanned for any signs of escape pods but found none. The Captain ordered the bridge crew to pinpoint the exact coordinates of the enemy ship's last known location. Once we arrived, I joined the physician and a squad of Kudra troopers on a Shuttlecraft mission to investigate what remained of the Roton's presence on the planet's surface.

As we descended onto the dusty terrain, our eyes swept over four lifeless Rotons scattered among debris and a damaged shuttlecraft. We cautiously disembarked from the shuttle and moved closer to examine the wreckage. However, just as we were about to approach the alien vessel, a figure emerged from behind a nearby boulder and signaled for us to stop. It was a human - a survivor or perhaps a traitor? We were unsure, but our instincts told us to proceed cautiously.

John's breath caught in his throat as he watched the small craft descend from the newly arrived, unidentified spaceship. It landed about 50 yards away from the damaged Bugheads' spacecraft, and five individuals dressed in military attire emerged, their guns ready. Three others in dark blue uniforms followed closely behind them. John could see the determination on their faces as they marched towards the alien landing craft. He knew these humans were likely from the ship that had destroyed the Bugheads' vessel. His heart raced as he saw the Bugheads crouched behind a nearby rock, poised for attack. Thinking quickly, John ran towards the approaching group, waving his arms frantically to communicate with them despite their language barrier. The Bugheads responded with clicking noises that echoed through the air, creating an eerie atmosphere. But John persisted, determined to warn these unsuspecting humans of the danger they were walking into.

As the group of humans turned to face him, they seemed confused but also grateful for the warning. However, before they could fully understand what was happening, the bugheads attacked from behind. John acted fast and took out the bugheads with one shot each, but not without receiving a painful laser burn on his left side. As he collapsed to the ground, he saw the Captain of their Starship rush over to him. She recognized that his warning had saved them from a deadly ambush.

The Captain and her crew quickly retrieved John and returned him to their ship for medical attention. John was surprised to see that all of them were female except for the doctor. Their advanced technology and skilled doctor allowed them to heal his burns within hours after fully recovering. John discovered that these women made up an all-female crew on a mission to find and destroy the deadly Rotons Planet Killer Ships. They invited John to join them on their journey, and he agreed without hesitation. After all, he had just experienced firsthand how incredible and brave these women were.

After the doctor had completed my treatment, the Captain learned that four enemy ships exited the Wormhole and headed toward them.

Our ship had limited resources: one laser fire control officer and two firing stations. The situation seemed dire, but the doctor had an idea. She suggested that I, with my light blue eyes, could potentially fill in as a Laser Control Officer. However, time was of the essence as the enemy ships would reach us in just 36 hours, leaving little time for extensive training. The doctor quickly devised a translation program for me to communicate effectively. With no other options available, the Captain asked me if I was willing to take on this responsibility. The Captain briefed me on the situation in light of the impending battle with four alien warships. She explained that we were short on laser fire control officers and asked if I would be willing to undergo training for the role. However, she made sure to mention the potential risks involved, including possible brain damage from multiple laser firings. The Captain stressed the gravity of my decision, given the limited time before the enemy ships arrived at our location. The chances of survival against four enemy ships were slim, but I was determined to seek revenge for the devastation on my home planet. The Captain then announced that I would be promoted to fleet officer and given the role of a Fire Control officer. She informed me I would join the fleet as the only male Fire Control officer among a 97% female-dominated force. As a recruit, I knew senior officers would closely monitor me, but my sole focus was seeking retribution for my people. I expressed my eagerness to begin training immediately, emphasizing my desire for vengeance. The Captain assigned Lieutenant Sar, a skilled laser Fire Control officer, to train me in preparation for battle.

To become fluent in the Galuten language, the doctor explained that I would have to take an educational program created by the ship's advanced computer system. The doctor escorted me to a room where I could relax in a chair while they attached wired probes to my head. After administering a calming injection and placing a helmet on my head, I drifted off into unconsciousness. When I woke up, it felt like only a short time had passed. The doctor entered the room and checked my well-being, letting me know I had been asleep for about two hours. Surprisingly, I could now understand everything she said in perfect Galuten. However, speaking and responding in this new language proved more difficult than expected. The doctor provided me with a digital pad programmed by the ship's computer specifically for the Galuten language to assist me with communication. With this device, I could communicate and comprehend in this foreign tongue.

I arrived at the designated time for a meeting in the Captain's conference room to discuss enlistment procedures. The Captain explained the process of joining the fleet, emphasizing that after forty years of service, I could become a citizen reserve or retire after seventy years with total compensation. The ship's computer translated the fleet officer's manual for me to review and sign on my pad. After carefully reading and signing the necessary documents, the Captain officially commissioned me to the rank of ensign. Thus begins my mission to seek revenge on the Rotons for the attack on my planet. Before concluding the meeting, the Captain addressed relationships on board the ship. She gave me four options: Female/Male, Male/Male, Female/ Female, or No Relationship. Having learned from my experience of being in a situation where relationships with fellow active duty personnel were not allowed, I chose the "No Relationship" option. The Captain noted that this choice may not sit well with the predominantly female crew (97%) but also acknowledged the challenges of extended patrols. She understood my perspective and asked if there were other topics to discuss before the meeting ended. I left with a sense of purpose and readiness to fulfill my duties as an officer while adhering to all regulations.

I informed the Captain that I needed to return to the landing site to complete an additional duty: caring for my fallen comrades. I reassured her that I would swiftly and efficiently complete the task. With her approval, I rushed to board the Shuttlecraft with the troopers, descending quickly to the designated landing site. We wasted no time; I hurried down the road to retrieve the Humbie while the troopers brought back the other two bodies. Maneuvering through dense foliage, I carried one comrade's body to the vehicle, only to realize that the troopers were already bringing the other two. As we gathered around the car's rear, I grabbed gas cans and poured fuel over the bodies. After signaling everyone to move back, I lit a match without hesitation. It was crucial to prevent our fallen soldiers from becoming prey to wild animals. Saying a prayer for their souls, I returned to the ship, knowing that I had fulfilled my duty of honoring and protecting my comrades in the best way possible.

After returning to the ship, Lieutenant Sar greeted me on the bridge, and we began our training session. Our first task was for me to familiarize myself with the fire control console and targeting helmet for our next mission. The console had a joystick for targeting, red buttons for firing lasers, and four other buttons for missiles, all neatly arranged. Our primary focus was practicing my aiming skills using the laser to hit simulated targets at various distances. I took out all the simulated targets from 2000 to 8000 yards away with precision and concentration. Lieutenant Sar was impressed by my accuracy and efficiency and reported it to the Captain. My sharp eyesight and mastery of the laser controls did not go unnoticed. Shortly after our training, we received a notification of an impending enemy encounter in four hours. The Captain instructed us to prepare for battle by being stationed at the firing pods.

THE EMPIRE FACED A difficult decision when implementing its advanced technology to automate its targeting system. Initially, the automated laser firing system gave them a clear advantage in battle, leading to many victories. However, their success was short-lived as the enemy discovered a way to send a signal back through the lasers, effectively disabling and destroying the automated system. It forced the Galuten fleet to use human operators to target the laser. Unfortunately, this solution came with its problems - only those with light-colored eyes could withstand the intense mental strain caused by the system's flashbacks. With only one in ten million people possessing such eye color in the Empire, recruiting individuals for this crucial role became increasingly difficult. Firing the lasers more than one time resulted in permanent brain damage, making it an unpopular and risky job within the fleet.

AS THE ALARM SOUNDED, I sprinted through the narrow corridors, my boots echoing on the steel floors. My heart pounded as I reached the launch bay and took my position with steady hands. Outside, the enemy fleet closed in, their sleek ships glittering in the starlight. Despite being outnumbered, we were ready for the battle ahead.

Our captain's voice filled my earpiece, reminding us to hold our fire until the enemy ships were closer distance away. But when they came within 8000 yards of us, I couldn't resist taking a calculated risk. I pulled the trigger, and an energy beam shot out of our ship, hitting one of the red ships and sending it into a fiery explosion. Two more ships met the same fate before Lieutenant Sar's skillful aim brought down the fourth ship. The odds were turning in our favor, but then one of the disabled ships fired two missiles at us. I intercepted and destroyed one of them quickly before it could do any damage. The second missile detonated too close to our hull, causing minor damage but reminding us of the constant danger in this intense battle for survival.

As the alarms blared and the lights flashed, I felt a sharp pain in my temples. The metal exterior of the spaceship had taken a hit, leaving a jagged hole in its hull. But inside, we were safe behind the sturdy, reinforced inner shell that protected us from potential dangers in space.

Amidst the chaos on the bridge, I noticed that Lieutenant Sar's pod was dark and silent. My heart sank as I rushed to her side, pushing through the panicked crew. Her body was limp as I lifted her into my arms and carried her to the medical center. The doctors told me that she was in a coma caused by the reflection of the laser during the attack. There was no way of knowing how long it would be before she woke up or what kind of damage had been done to her brain. But none of that mattered to me. Lieutenant Sar had trained me, creating a solid bond. All that mattered now was her recovery. I refused to leave her side, even as the days turned weeks and months. I held her hand, talked, and stayed by her bedside. And finally, she opened her eyes after what seemed like an eternity. The relief and joy I felt was indescribable. She still had a long road ahead of her, but I knew that with my unwavering support by her side, she would make a full recovery. Our bond grew stronger during those difficult times, and I am grateful for every moment we spent together fighting for her survival.

While the lieutenant recovered from her injuries, the ship's doctor informed me that she needed to run tests on my mental state. After firing multiple lasers, the Empire discovered it caused significant brain damage in most personnel. However, I seemed to be an exception as I had fired four beams without damage. The diagnostic results showed no mental impairment, only a minor headache. Pope, though, might have been due to my DNA being 93.5% different from Galuten DNA and having received laser eye surgery from the army. As for Lieutenant Sar, she woke up from her coma but had sustained 11% brain damage, which prevented her from continuing as a Fire Control officer. The lieutenant took it well and said I will return to navigation. When she asked if I had been by her side while she was unconscious, I reassured her that I was there to make sure the lieutenant was okay and that she was my only friend on the ship. I encouraged her to get some rest and promised we would talk later. We successfully destroyed all four enemy ships and completed our mission. The Captain's voice was concerned as she advised me to rest well before we entered the Wormhole. The countdown on the control panel blinked red, signaling that we had only 36 hours until our journey through the wormhole began. My heart raced with excitement and trepidation as I made my way to my quarters, knowing that the adventure ahead would test my physical endurance and mental fortitude. The anticipation of what lay beyond the Wormhole kept me up long into the night, but eventually, exhaustion took over, and I drifted off into a restless sleep, dreaming of distant galaxies and new frontiers.

Chapter 2

After a brief rest, during which I went over my previous experiences, I resolved to venture back to the NCO mess hall for a meal, hopeful for a more favorable encounter. However, it quickly became apparent that the senior NCOs had some reservations about ensigns sharing their space, as only those with the rank of Lieutenant or higher had access to the officer's mess. En route to the mess hall, The crew met me with warm greetings from several crew members, their smiles accompanied by a peculiar gesture involving two raised fingers. While a single-finger gesture might carry an explicit indication back on Earth, the meaning behind this two-finger salute remained a mystery, prompting me to make a mental note for further investigation upon stepping into the mess hall. I was surprised by the sight of a standing salute, Which I promptly returned. As I made my way to collect my meal, the other diners graciously made room for me at their table. I sat opposite the most senior NCO, who greeted me warmly and expressed gratitude for my service to our ship. The meal was a delightful surprise, boasting flavors and textures entirely novel to my palate, offering a taste of the exotic and unfamiliar. After exchanging briefly with my fellow diners, I went to the bridge to confer with the Captain. I approached the Captain with a request to return to my base to retrieve personal belongings. To my relief, the Captain granted my request and arranged for a shuttle pilot, two troopers, and an individual storage unit to accompany me.

Our journey took us approximately 5 miles south of our original landing site, where I gathered various items essential to my comfort and duty. Among these were additional M35 rifles, a 9-millimeter pistol, two cases of ammunition, clothing, uniforms, and my computer and memory disk containing a vast library of backed-up movies and TV shows. Upon returning to the ship with my belongings, I felt grateful for the Captain's understanding and support. It was a reminder of the mutual respect underpinning our shared mission aboard the vessel.

After maintenance completed inspecting the hall and ensuring the ship was in good condition, the maintenance crew signaled the green light for our return journey to their home world. Aware of the impending voyage, the Captain swiftly prepared the ship accordingly. As we embarked on our journey through the wormholes, I seized the opportunity to learn about Galeton, my soon-to-be home with which I was eager to acquaint myself. Utilizing the ship's computer, I delved into valuable insights about Galeton. I discovered that Galeton was integral to a vast and sprawling civilization known as the Empire, spanning numerous star systems and planets. At the heart of this Empire lay the capital planet, Galuten. Galuton predominantly comprised untamed wilderness, with sixty percent of its surface covered in water, while the remainder was farmland. Notably, the Planet boasted a solitary major city, housing an approximate population of eight million inhabitants. Governed by a hereditary line of powerful Empresses wielding significant influence over their subjects, the Empire spanned 21 star systems, each with habitable planets, overseen by a hereditary line of Barraness. Innovation and progress are highly prized by this society, with the Empress's reign characterized by a strict order extending throughout the galaxy. Just as I contemplated visiting the doctor to address some concerns, a summons from the Captain diverted my attention. The purpose of the meeting, held in her conference room, was to discuss the fleet bonus program explicitly tailored for laser control officers like myself. Throughout the meeting,

She provided me with a written list to ensure all pertinent details were thoroughly understood and accounted for.

<u>*FLEET BONUS PROGRAM FOR LASER CONTROL OFFICER*</u>
<u>*Bonus Report #1 For John Pope*</u>

1. *Three enemy ships destroyed 35,000* Quills*x 4 =105,000* Quills.

The present Bonus Total is 105,000 Quills.

THE FLEET HAD NOT ANTICIPATED the necessity of providing bonuses to any laser control officer, deeming it nearly impossible to reach such bonus levels. The Empire is bound by policy to compensate you according to the bounty policy. The Captain remarked, "You're fortunate to be entitled to such a generous bonus. Given your exceptional laser-firing proficiency without mental repercussions, the Empire might reconsider its policy. This policy aimed to incentivize fleet officers with light-colored eyes to pursue the position of laser Fire Control officer despite the inherent risk of mental strain during firing sequences. Expressing gratitude to the Captain for the insight, I acknowledged my lack of understanding regarding Quill's value. I resolved to ascertain its worth when making purchases in the future. "Ensign Pope." "Yes, captain." "I suggest you tour the ship to get familiar with the layout." "I will do that right away, captain."

I started my exploration by inspecting the ship's compartments, beginning with the bridge situated at the forefront of the vessel, housing all controls along with two laser firing pods on the right and left side. Progressing towards the ship's rear, I encountered the Captain's conference room, succeeded by the Captain's cabin. I found senior officers' quarters to the left side while the officers' mess further down on the right. On the opposite side, the ensigns' quarters were located across from the crew mess's entrance, accommodating the NCO section. Continuing along the left side, I encountered the maintenance area and the spare parts department. At the far end of the corridor lay the entrance to the Stardrive systems. Below the deck, a storage area was present alongside sections dedicated to extra missiles—two missile firing pods and two laser-generating systems on the lower deck.

While navigating the intricate layout of the ship, I unexpectedly crossed paths with Lieutenant Row, prompting me to suggest sharing a cup of coffee to foster a deeper connection. With mutual agreement, we ventured to the mess hall, savored the aromatic warmth of freshly brewed coffee, and engaged in conversation. During our dialogue, I couldn't resist inquiring about Lieutenant Rowe's deliberate choice to pursue the role of a laser-firing Control officer, fully aware of the potential risks associated with such a position, particularly the threat of brain damage. To my surprise, she told me her decision to show her independence from her mother's objection, a distinguished Starship captain who instilled profound admiration for the fleet. Despite her mother's initial disapproval, Lieutenant Rowe boldly opted for the laser-control officer path, driven by a desire to assert her independence and set her destiny within the vast expanse of the fleet. In exchange, I felt compelled to unveil my motivations for volunteering as a laser-control officer. I confessed that my Planet and its innocent inhabitants had fallen victim to the ruthless destruction wrought by alien beings. Driven by an unwavering thirst for justice and a desire for revenge, I willingly embraced the position, viewing it as an opportunity to confront and destroy those responsible for the devastation of my home world. I also shared my intrigue about the Captain's age, making an educated guess that she appeared to be approximately 24 years old, which left me shocked at the thought of such a young individual commanding a massive starship. However, my surprise quickly turned into skepticism when Lieutenant Rowe, smiling, revealed, "The captain's actual age is around 140 years old." She explained the wonders of genetic manipulation and a rejuvenation process through which individuals in this society could defy the boundaries of time and live significantly longer lives. It's surprising to discover that the captain, despite her youthful appearance, is actually 140 years old. All the women on this ship are in excellent condition. They are not too tall, not too short, not too fat, and not too thin. How is that possible? They all look like they could be models or movie stars. How can a society be so perfect? I'm going to have to do some more research on everything I see right in front of my eyes.

After my coffee break with Lieutenant Row, I headed to the ship's medical department to discuss with the doctor the potential impacts of genetic manipulation on Galuten society. I intended to delve into the possibility of creating individuals free from any imperfections or flaws. The doctor told me," A group of scientists and geneticists had embarked on a courageous mission to engineer a flawless and resilient population genetically. Utilizing cutting-edge genetic technologies, they aimed to eliminate diseases, enhance intelligence, and establish a society that was overall healthier and more robust. Despite their ambitious goals, the scientists were not oblivious to the risks and downsides associated with altering the genetic makeup of society. They were well aware that there could be unforeseen consequences stemming from manipulating the human genome, and this awareness led them to proceed with caution in their endeavors."

The societal dynamics underwent profound changes due to genetic modifications, triggering unforeseen transformations. With genetically enhanced attributes, women ascended as the dominant force, assuming leadership positions, while men gravitated towards academia and science. This unique role division challenged traditional gender norms within the Galuten Empire. Women became protectors and governors in galactic society, reshaping the power landscape. However, this manipulation also catalyzed a decline in the birth rate, resulting in a modest population of 8 million on the central Planet. Consequently, replenishing the population became daunting amidst this decline, prompting the Empire to confront new challenges in maintaining its societal structure and sustainability.

Following a consultation with the physician, I decided to head towards the recreational and gym area. Upon entering, I saw troopers engrossed in hand-to-hand combat training. Intrigued by their intense regimen, I observed from the sidelines. Soon, the trooper Lieutenant noticed my interest and, recognizing my combat veteran status, invited me to participate alongside one of her top contenders. Eager to refine my skills, I accepted.

Paired with the Lieutenant's most skilled trooper, we engaged in a lengthy sparring session. While impressed by her proficiency, I noted a few openings for potential takedowns. However, I refrained from exploiting them out of respect and to avoid embarrassment. After the session, I thanked the trooper for the opportunity. Surprisingly, she astutely observed that I seemed to be holding back, suggesting mutual benefit in addressing weaknesses and enhancing our combat skills in future sessions. Her insight resonated with me, and I appreciated her push towards improvement. The Lieutenant also expressed gratitude for my participation and promised to inform me of future practice sessions. With a sense of accomplishment, I returned to my room, reflecting on the day's events. The experience showcased the troopers' dedication and allowed me to hone my skills. Grateful for learning from such skilled individuals, I eagerly anticipated future sessions where we could push each other to new heights.

THE STARSHIP TROOPERS hailed from the planet Xerion-9, governed by a rigid military regime. The society there bore a unique hallmark: an exclusive focus on producing an all-female fighting force, the troopers. These formidable warriors have unparalleled combat prowess, discipline, and unswerving allegiance to their Empire. From tender years, troopers underwent rigorous training in specialized academies, where they honed expertise in diverse martial arts, mastered advanced weaponry, and crafted strategic acumen. Their mandate was clear: furnish the Empire with an elite cadre equipped to confront the most grueling combat scenarios. The troopers are indispensable to the Empire, entrusted with maintaining peace and upholding its laws across vast expanses of space, symbolizing strength, honor, duty, and sacrifice. Whether patrolling borders, engaging in interstellar conflicts, or executing covert operations, they stood as vanguards of the Empire's supremacy, stalwart safeguarding its interests and projecting its influence throughout the Empire.

I WAS SUMMONED TO THE Captain's conference room and briefed on my new assignment. At the head of the table, the Captain informed me that it was my duty to operate the alarm and security consoles on the bridge as part of my regular duties during our transit. In addition to this crucial role, she underscored the significance of my duty to operate the laser-firing pod control whenever we approached a wormhole transfer point. Aware of the potential peril lurking in these transfer points, the Captain stressed the gravity of the situation: it fell on me to swiftly neutralize any hostile vessels that threatened our ship and crew. The responsibility settled heavily upon me as I absorbed the Captain's words. It was clear that my actions could mean the difference between our safe passage through the void and confrontation with enemy forces. With resolve and determination, I pledged to uphold my duties with vigilance and dedication, safeguarding our vessel and its precious cargo as we traversed the wormholes.

As we approached the first wormhole transfer point, I climbed into the cockpit of the laser-firing Pod. My hands gripped the controls tightly as I scanned the darkness for signs of danger. Suddenly, a yellow vessel emerged from the shadows. I saw a missile hurtling toward us. Reacting quickly, I fired my lasers and took out the missile just in time. But our attacker wasn't done yet. They retaliated with a barrage of plasma fire that lit up the darkness around us. I maneuvered our ship, dodging the blasts while firing back at our foe. I set all fear aside as I focused on defending our crew and ship. My shots only caused minimal damage to the enemy's shields, but I remained determined. Adjusting my aim, I targeted their star drive with two precise shots. The resulting hits shattered the pirate vessel into countless fragments, sending them tumbling into the void. As I scanned for any remaining threats, relief washed over me as no life pods appeared on my screen. The Captain congratulated me on my success and told me there was a substantial bounty of 35,000 Quills for taking down such a formidable adversary. With our path finally clear, we entered the wormhole that would take us back to Galuten Prime. As we traveled through space, I couldn't help but feel proud and grateful for being able to protect and serve alongside my fellow crew members.

Now that we were on our way, I stood at my post, monitoring the alarm and security console. The Captain entered the bridge, instantly commanding the attention and respect of the entire crew. With each crew member snapping to attention, it was clear that they were ready and prepared for any situation. As she approached me, the Captain addressed me as Ensign Pope, acknowledging my role as a skilled Laser Control Officer. In her address to the crew, she praised my quick and decisive actions that destroyed three enemy Roton ships and a lurking Raider vessel at the wormhole transfer point, effectively preventing an ambush. "It was evident that our mission could have been in serious jeopardy without his expertise in laser control. In recognition of his performance," the Captain proudly announced a well-deserved promotion, promoting me to the rank of Lieutenant. The Captain presented me with the emblem of a Lieutenant, symbolizing my newly acquired rank. In response to the Captain's announcement, I rendered a crisp salute, expressing my appreciation for the honor given me through this promotion. This promotion reminded me of the trust and confidence the Captain had placed in me. Our journey was coming to an end. The moment the ship emerged from the wormhole, a surge of expectation went through me, marking my official arrival at the center of the Galuten Empire. Having recently enlisted in the Empire's fleet, I was utterly captivated by the grandeur unfolding in the Empire's home Star system. Our exit from the wormhole revealed a vast expanse of space stretched out before us, with planets orbiting around the central star, with a Planet that housed the seat of imperial power. I couldn't help but feel a mixture of wonder and apprehension as I realized I was now a part of the formidable force that governed this expansive galaxy. The journey through the wormhole had brought me to the core of the Empire, where my duties and destiny awaited me. Despite the uncertainty of what lay ahead, I knew I was now a piece in the intricate puzzle that shaped the galaxy's fate.

On our journey toward the primary Planet, the Captain paused to relay to the crew that our vessel would be docking at station 50 for hull repairs and necessary maintenance. She informed the crew that they would have a well-deserved break lasting around two weeks, reminding them to keep their communication devices nearby. The Captain told them their com unit would notified when it was time to return to the ship. The Captain told me she would accompany me to the fleet administration office on the shuttle. Once we arrived, I could acquire my identification and debit ID card and receive new dress uniforms and clothing items.

Upon arrival at the administration office, I received my combination ID, debit card, and smartwatch com device. Proceeding to the uniform section, I underwent a thorough sizing process. I Positioned myself on a state-of-the-art scanner that could take measurements to craft my personalized clothing. The procedure was estimated to be around one hour. The automated Taylor would prepare my custom-made attire. The uniform was a deep shade of blue, adorned with my Lieutenant badges on the shoulders, a laser fire control badge on the right side, and my name embroidered on the left. As the Captain bid me farewell, she provided information regarding the available accommodation options. She gave me a choice between staying in the bachelor officer's quarters in the nearby building or selecting a hotel in the vibrant city center. Expressing my appreciation for her guidance, I assured her I would decide once I received my uniforms.

Opting to explore the city, I headed towards the front gate and boarded a waiting transport. Once inside, I instructed the driver to take me to a hotel in the city's heart. Upon reaching the hotel, I proceeded to the front desk to complete the check-in process. The desk clerk, aware of the hotel's reputation, suggested a more budget-friendly option for my stay. I handed over my ID and debit card so he could check for room availability, balance verification, and necessary arrangements. While the clerk was busy with the verification process, I noticed another clerk whispering something to the hotel manager while pointing in my direction. Intrigued by this, I wondered what could be the matter. The manager, recognizing me as Lieutenant John Pope, approached with a warm smile and expressed her delight in having me as a guest at their establishment. She commended my heroic actions as a Laser Fire control officer, which had made headlines for saving my ship.

To show their appreciation, the manager generously offered me a complimentary upgrade to a deluxe room and extended an invitation to dine at the hotel's restaurant at seven pm, believing the other guests would be thrilled to have me there. She assured me that an automated room server would assist me with my luggage and escort me to my room. The room is remarkable, and after a tiring day, I took some much-needed rest. It was a long and exhausting day, and the comfort of the room was a welcome respite. I set my watch to remind me when it was time for dinner, ensuring I wouldn't miss the opportunity to indulge in a free meal.

After a refreshing and good rest, I proceeded to the hotel's top restaurant. A nearby family came to my attention as the gracious host escorted me to my designated table. Among them sat a young girl, her eyes brimming with curiosity and a sense of awe. Approaching their table with a genuine smile, I warmly greeted the family and wished them a pleasant evening. The little girl's eyes widened with excitement when she discovered my profession as a distinguished fleet starship officer. Filled with enthusiasm, she eagerly shared her dream of becoming a starship officer. I realized the impact I could have on her aspirations and left her with a lasting memento. With utmost care, I reached into my uniform and retrieved my hat, gently placing it on her head while saying, "For the aspiring starship officer." The girl's face instantly lit up joyfully, creating a heartwarming moment. After enjoying a delightful dinner, I bid the family farewell. I made my way back to my room, already envisioning the exciting exploration of the city on foot that awaited me the following day. As I reflected on the day's events, my mind drifted back to my childhood on the farm. The memories of tending to the land alongside my father were etched deep within me, instilling a sense of responsibility and connection to the Earth despite my youthful rebellion against farm life's predictability. The transition from farmhand to soldier was abrupt and challenging, yet it ignited a sense of purpose. I embraced the rigorous training and discipline of military life, driven by a desire to make a difference and protect those unable to defend themselves. Little did I know that my journey would lead me beyond the confines of Earth and into the vast expanse of space.

Joining the Galactic Empire's fleet was an experience, a far cry from the fields of my youth. Yet, as I navigated the intricacies of life aboard the starship, I found myself drawing upon the values instilled in me by my father: integrity and a deep respect for life in all its forms. As I settled into my room for the night, surrounded by the quiet hum of the city beyond, I couldn't help but feel a sense of gratitude for the journey that had brought me here. Each step and decision led me closer to this moment, where I was on the precipice of a new chapter in my life. Tomorrow held the promise of new adventures and challenges, yet for now, I allowed myself to bask in the warmth of the present moment. With a contented sigh, I switched off the light and settled into sleep, the anticipation of tomorrow's possibilities in my mind. Little did I know that the coming days would test me in ways I never imagined, pushing me to the limits of my strength and resolve. But for now, I allowed myself to savor the stillness of the night, knowing that whatever the future held, I was ready to face it head-on.

As dawn broke over the city skyline, I awoke to the gentle hum of the city coming to life. Stretching out on the plush bedding, I couldn't help but feel excited for the day ahead. Today, I marked the beginning of my exploration of this vibrant metropolis, a chance to immerse myself in its culture and history. After a leisurely breakfast at the hotel's dining area, I set out to discover the city's hidden gems. Stepping out onto the bustling streets, I saw that the air was alive with the aroma of freshly brewed coffee and the chatter of passersby going about their day.

With no particular destination in mind, I allowed myself to wander, allowing the city's rhythm to guide my footsteps. Found quaint cafes tucked away in cobblestone alleys to bustling markets. As I strolled along the winding streets, I couldn't help but marvel at the city's rich tapestry of history and culture. Each building bore the scars of time, a testament to the resilience of its inhabitants in the face of adversity. It reminded us of the enduring spirit that bound us together, regardless of our origins or backgrounds. Lost in the city's labyrinth, I stumbled upon a quaint bookstore between towering skyscrapers. Intrigued by the promise of literary treasures within, I felt the musty scent as I stepped inside. It was the fragrance of old books. Rows upon shelves lined the walls, each overflowing with books. As I perused the shelves, I saw a weathered book tucked away in a forgotten corner. Its faded cover bore the title "Tales of the Galactic Frontier," a collection of stories from the far reaches of the cosmos. Intrigued, I pulled the book from its resting place and settled into a nearby armchair, eager to lose myself in its pages. It was a welcome escape from the hustle and bustle of city life, a chance to immerse myself in the wonders of the imagination. As the sun descended below the horizon, casting long shadows across the city streets, I reluctantly tore myself away from the book and emerged back into the bustling city. It was a day of adventure and discovery, leaving me with a newfound appreciation for the beauty and diversity of the city. As I returned to the hotel, the day's events replayed in my mind, each moment etched into my memory like the pages of a beloved book. Tomorrow held the promise of new experiences and adventures, yet for now, I allowed myself to bask in the warmth of the present moment, grateful for the opportunity to explore this vast and wondrous city. With a contented sigh, I slipped beneath the soft covers of my bed, exhaustion weighing down my limbs from the day's adventures. My mind was buzzing with memories and thoughts, refusing to let go. As sleep finally claimed me, I eagerly surrendered myself to the realm of dreams, curious and excited for what tomorrow would bring. The gentle hum of the air conditioner provided a soothing backdrop, lulling me deeper into a peaceful slumber.

Chapter 3

I decided to take a leisurely walk around the city again, the opportunity to immerse myself in the urban city. As he moved through the streets, his inquisitive nature was immediately captivated by the sight of a large gathering of people outside a majestic building. Determined to uncover the reason behind this gathering, he approached a nearby onlooker with a courteous nod, initiating a conversation to unravel the mystery. The bystander, with an air of anticipation, eagerly shared the purpose of the crowd: the imminent Appearance of the High Priestess of the Church of Faith. The rare occurrence had drawn crowds of admirers, all eager to glimpse her presence. Intrigued by the prospect of witnessing such an event, Lieutenant Pope deliberated his next move. Should he immerse himself in the crowd's excitement, joining them in anticipation of the High Priestess's appearance? Or should I continue his solitary journey through the streets of the city? As Lieutenant Pope weighed his options, he couldn't shake the allure of the rare spectacle unfolding before him. The energy of the crowd, coupled with the anticipation of witnessing the High Priestess's presence

Pope joining the crowd would offer him a unique opportunity to experience a moment to witness the figure of the High Priestess. On the other hand, continuing his solitary exploration would grant him the freedom to wander at his own pace, allowing him to absorb the city's essence. Ultimately, after a moment of reflection, Pope made his decision. He chose to venture into the heart of the crowd. Pope pushed through the crowd confidently to get to the front line. As he reached his destination, a woman emerged from the building, commanding the attention of everyone present with her striking beauty and refined aura. She greeted the onlookers with friendly gestures and a warm smile, instantly spreading joy among the crowd.

Suddenly, chaos erupted. A cry pierced through the air, signaling the presence of a dangerous individual wielding a laser weapon. He quickly diverted his gaze and saw that the target was none other than the High Priestess herself. Without hesitation, he leaped into action and positioned himself between her and the incoming laser strike, determined to shield her from harm. The searing heat of the laser hit him in the upper right shoulder, and he fell to the ground in pain.

The crowd swarmed around the assailant, taking her down before she could do any more damage. As she lay unconscious on the ground, the High Priestess took control of the situation with ease and authority. Her calm voice said, "Take care of the officer first." Her clear instructions and composed demeanor instilled a sense of order in those around her. "Make sure Doctor Woran attends to him in the medical section without delay," she added, emphasizing the situation's urgency. The Doctor and the medical team attended to the Pope's injuries. They positioned him on a specialized medical bed with precision and care, prioritizing his comfort and stability. Led by the capable Dr. Woran, a team of seasoned assistants promptly sprang into action. The Doctor assumed command, directing the staff to conduct a thorough examination to gauge the extent of the laser-induced injuries. In a display of coordination, they swiftly procured a scanning device and assessed Lieutenant Pope's internal condition. Thankfully, the monitor displayed no significant harm to his vital organs. However, the laser burns demanded urgent attention. With urgency, the medical staff prepared for Lieutenant Pope's transfer to the regeneration unit. They carefully moved him to the specialized chamber, where cutting-edge technology would work magic. As the regeneration process commenced, the chamber hummed with activity, promising to mend the damaged tissue. Amidst the activity, the High Priestess watched closely, her concern evident in her gaze. Yet, amidst the tension, a sense of hope filled the room, bolstered by the Doctor's expertise and the medical team's dedication.

The medical department informed the fleet about the incident leading to his injuries. In reaction, a fleet doctor arrived to evaluate the medical procedures done on him. After assessing the quality of care he received, all parties agreed to leave his continued treatment in the hands of the current medical team. Nevertheless, they asked for regular updates on his recovery.

After approximately 24 hours, the medical team extracted him from the regeneration process. Upon awakening in the CCU unit, the Doctor told him the regeneration was successful, but he would likely experience soreness for some time. During a body scan, medical professionals discovered at least seven fragments of metal near vital organs. They presented him with the option of removing these fragments to prevent potential damage to his system. He informed them these metal pieces were remnants from a combat mission where a nearby mine exploded. However, during the initial incident, the medical department deemed it too risky to remove the scrap metal due to its proximity to vital organs. The medical department notified the fleet regarding the discovery of the metal fragments they would like to remove. Fleet sent a doctor to assess the medical protocols for his treatment. He evaluated the quality of care he was receiving, and together, they agreed to leave his continued therapy in the hands of the current medical team. However, they requested periodic updates on his progress and recovery. Pope informed that the current medical team possessed the expertise to extract the particles and asked if he wanted to proceed with the removal. In response, he expressed his willingness, "Since he came this far with the treatment, it was best to complete the job."

Moments later, I saw this odd-looking device beside me in the operating room. The Doctor, now accompanied by a team of technicians, explained the machine was equipped with advanced precision and capabilities beyond human skill, making it ideal for delicate procedures. Despite my instinctive urge to voice my concerns, They swiftly sedated me, leaving me with no choice. The robotic surgeon began its meticulous work, navigating through my body to locate and remove the troublesome metal fragments. As it worked, I couldn't shake the surreal feeling of being operated on by a machine rather than a human. The robotic surgeon worked tirelessly, and its movements were precise and calculated. The medical team monitored the procedure closely, their attention shifting between screens displaying vital signs and the intricate visuals from the surgeon's cameras. Eventually, the robotic arms carefully extracted the last metal fragment. The procedure was a success. As I regained consciousness, the Doctor explained the details of the operation and reassured me the robotic surgeon's precision minimized any potential risks. While I couldn't deny the technological marvel saved me from the burden of those metal fragments, a part of me couldn't help but reflect on the changing landscape of medicine. As I recovered, I pondered what difference living in this society would be from Earth. Later, the Doctor entered my room. She presented me with a bottle containing the seven metal fragments extracted from my body. Inquiring if I wanted to keep them, I disposed of them instead, as they only reminded me of a distressing memory I wished to forget.

After a few days in recovery, as I prepared to leave, a representative of the high priestess approached me, requesting I accompany her as the high priestess wished to meet me in her quarters. She welcomed me with a friendly smile and invited me to sit. Expressing gratitude for saving her life, the high priestess mentioned the potential of an extraordinary gift she would like to give me. She then reached for a box, unveiling a peculiar-looking laser pistol. Describing it as a discovery from an archaeological site, her organization was excavating on a planet linked to an ancient race that was no longer present in this part of the Galaxy. She said the empire granted permission for the removal and sale of artifacts. These items would be sold to museums and collectors throughout the Galaxy, with the proceeds dedicated to supplying medical and food resources for her to help the less fortunate across the empire's star systems. She began to explain the remarkable capabilities of the weapon, fully aware of the doubt it might evoke. She extended her arm, and to my amazement, a laser pistol materialized seemingly out of thin air. For a moment, time became suspended as I beheld the sight before me. Then, just as swiftly as it had appeared, the pistol vanished, leaving me in disbelief at the phenomenon I had just witnessed. She proceeded to expound upon the nature of her newfound ability. With each word, the mystery deepened, captivating my imagination. She described how, through mere touch, the laser pistol could be summoned into existence, defying all conventional understanding. She elaborated further, recounting instances where the gun had come to her aid in moments of need or danger as though it possessed a sense of its purpose. Its Appearance was not arbitrary but rather a response to the situation's urgency. It dematerializes back into who knows where.

, disappearing into another dimension beyond our comprehension. The notion of a weapon with such capabilities challenged the boundaries of rationality, yet the Highpristes' words had an undeniable sense of truth. I drew deeper into this extraordinary phenomenon, with the implications of its existence and the questions it raised. "I wanted you to be aware of all the facts before offering it to you. I believe you would utilize it for good purposes rather than evil ones. Let me know if you're interested in taking possession of it." Appreciating the transparency, I expressed my interest, explaining that as a combat infantry soldier, such a tool would greatly aid in carrying out my duties. I thanked the priestess for the Laser Gun gift. Upon receiving the laser pistol and replicating the same act she demonstrated, my curiosity led me to inquire about its recharge mechanism. She assured me the gun consistently returned fully charged each time it was employed. Emphasizing the extraordinary nature of the weapon, she noted the technology embedded within it surpassed anything currently within our possession.

To my astonishment, she caught me off guard by extending an invitation to join her for dinner, emphasizing it was getting late and we could enjoy a meal together. Undoubtedly, The offer was too generous to decline, especially considering how mesmerized I was by this intriguing and stunning woman. As we enjoyed our meal, our conversation naturally gravitated toward my life on my home planet. She inquired about my life and whether I had a female companion on our home planet. I interpreted her question as asking about my marital status and whether a spouse awaited me back home. I told her that, as a combat soldier, I understood the weight of my deployment on a potential partner and its challenges. I could not lay that kind of burden on anyone. She expressed gratitude for my consideration. As we proceeded with a pleasant conversation and the time grew late, I became more and more effectuated by this beautiful woman seated across from me. As we stood up, she approached me, grabbed my hand, and said follow me. We proceeded to the next room, which appeared to be a bedroom. We entered the bedroom, and she closed the door. We leave the rest of the night to your imagination as a gentleman.

The following day, we shared breakfast, and unexpectedly. My watch com alert system signaled me to return to my ship. Expressing my gratitude for all she and her organization had done for me, I assured her our encounter would forever remain etched in my memory. In return, she expressed her appreciation once more for saving her life, planted a kiss on my cheek, and bid me goodbye. I returned to the shuttle port for the trip to Space Station 50 to board my ship. The whirlwind of events that had transpired during the evening consumed

Pope. The encounter with the High Priestess had left an indelible mark on him, her captivating presence lingering in his thoughts long after their intimate exchange. He became acutely aware of the need to delve deeper into the mysteries that surrounded this intriguing woman. John instinctively reached for his notepad and swiftly connected the Wi-Fi, embarking on a determined investigation to unearth more information about the High Priestess. The screen displayed the following info.

NAME: SOLARIA HIGH Priestess Age: Estimated to be in her mid to late 60s Appearance: an ethereal beauty with piercing eyes that seem to hold wisdom. Her demeanor is graceful and poised, and she moves purposefully and powerfully.

1. The High Priestess is a mysterious and enigmatic figure shrouded in secrecy about her origins and past. Rumors swirl about her potential training in remote monasteries within the empire, adding to the mystique that surrounds her persona.

2. Within the Church of Faith, the High Priestess holds a revered position, known for her spiritual guidance and profound insights that she imparts to her followers. Her role as a spiritual leader is highly respected and sought after by many.

3. The High Priestess wields a significant influence, commanding a loyal following of disciples who seek her wisdom and guidance in various aspects of life, whether mundane or esoteric. Leaders, scholars, and truth-seekers seek her counsel, highlighting her importance in the community.

AS JOHN DELVED DEEPER into his research, he realized that uncovering the truth about the High Priestess would require more than gathering information. It would demand intuition and a willingness to confront the unknown. With a resolve strengthened by curiosity and intrigue, he set out to unravel the veiled mysteries surrounding the woman who had come into his life.

As I went through the check-in process, I made it explicitly clear that I preferred not to have any partners. Commander Yayka warmly welcomed me and informed me we had a new Captain, Captain Xala, as Captain Chrone was on leave. However, He cautioned about the new Captain's formidable reputation, which made me apprehensive. Once I settled into my cabin, I received an unexpected call instructing me to report to the Captain immediately. I made my way to her dayroom, where she awaited me. The Captain wasted no time and requested that I modify my partner's statistics. However, I politely declined, reminding her that fleet regulations strictly prohibited anyone from ordering me to make such changes. Unfortunately, my refusal didn't sit well with her, and she warned me that the journey ahead could be quite challenging. I couldn't help but interpret her words as a veiled threat, leaving me uneasy about what would come.

Upon reaching their destination, Captain Xela, seeking revenge, assigned Lieutenant Pope to accompany an undersized unit of troopers as an observer on a dangerous mission on planet Tarorn. Their objective is to thwart an uprising to overthrow the local authorities despite being vastly outnumbered. The primary goal is to delay the government's fall until reinforcements reach them. Little did Captain Xala know that Lieutenant Pope was not just an observer but a highly skilled combat infantry veteran with extensive training. As they face a daunting 20 to 1 numerical disadvantage against the local rebel forces, the mission takes on a suicidal nature. The stakes are high, as we must defend the government at all costs. The government's survival hangs in the balance, and the mission's success hinges on the team's ability to lead the troopers effectively in the face of overwhelming odds. Holding off the rebels until reinforcements arrive is crucial. Lieutenant Pope and the Troopers face the ultimate test in this life-threatening encounter.

Pope and the Troopers faced a rebel force that vastly outnumbered them, requiring them to depend on their strategic understanding and military expertise to stand a chance at achieving victory. Pope and the Trooper Major devised a plan to deceive the enemy in collaboration. Instead of deploying their entire force conventionally, they decided to reposition their troops strategically. Not only did they position them at the front, but they also cleverly placed them on both sides of the rebels. The objective was to create an illusion to make the enemy believe they were facing a much larger force. By spreading their troops across multiple directions, Pope and the Troopers aimed to stretch the perception of the rebel force, making it appear as though they were being confronted from the front and flanked. This tactical maneuver sows confusion, hesitation, and doubt among the rebel ranks. Pope and the troopers understood their strength in this situation lay not only in their numbers but also in their ability to deceive. Pope acknowledged his responsibility for the plan and hoped everything worked out for the best. He addressed the unit to say, "We will leave no one behind wounded or dead, I promise." As the rebels approached, they met with an unexpected sight - not a straightforward confrontation, but rather a meticulously planned deception of a larger and more formidable force. The success of this maneuver hinged on the rebels falling for the visual deception, which would grant Pope and his troopers a crucial advantage in the upcoming battle. The insurgents, caught off guard as the assault commenced, encountered gunfire from three directions. To regroup, they swiftly retreated to reassess their position. Even though we endured a significant loss of 50% casualties, their retreat bought us enough time for reinforcements to arrive. The delay proved to be crucial in turning the tide of the battle. When the reinforcements finally arrived, the local insurgents faced a well-prepared and reinforced opponent.

The uprising sought to overthrow the local authorities, but it failed, and the government on Planet Tarorn stood firm. Though the troopers suffered heavy casualties, there were no deaths among them. The hazardous mission came at a high cost, but it quelled the uprising and preserved the order on Planet. The wounded soldiers were taken to the Havey cruiser for medical care while the remaining group members returned to Star Ship 35. Upon arrival, Commander Yayka greeted us and asked for a private discussion with me. She revealed she had taken on the role of acting Captain, as the original Captain Xala sent to the heavy cruiser on the orders of Admiral Astraea. The Admiral wanted to see me and waited in the Captain's day room. I thanked the commander for the update and proceeded to Admiral Astra's location. Upon entering the Captain's day room, the Admiral welcomed me warmly, calling me Lieutenant Pope and expressing relief at my safe return. She noted that I should not have been part of a combat mission, given my crucial role as the sole Laser Fire Control officer in the entire fleet. In response, She had the Captain relieved of command due to her actions in this manner. I detailed how my experience as a combat infantryman enabled me to offer valuable support to the team. "Your assistance during the mission was outstanding and greatly valued by the empire." The Admiral smiled and advised me to freshen up and rest as we returned home. I saluted respectfully and exited the bridge, ready to prepare for our journey back.

As Lieutenant Pope prepared for the journey back, he couldn't shake the memories of the recent mission on Planet Tarorn. The successful quelling of the uprising had come at a cost, leaving him with a newfound sense of camaraderie with his fellow troopers. Despite the heavy casualties, the mission underscored the importance of teamwork and strategic thinking in adversity. As he settled into his quarters aboard Star Ship 35, Lieutenant Pope took a moment to reflect on the events that had transpired since his encounter with the High Priestess. The gift of the laser pistol served as a constant reminder of the extraordinary circumstances that had brought them together. He marveled at the weapon's capabilities, pondering the implications of its existence in a universe filled with technological marvels. Lost in thought, Lieutenant Pope couldn't help but wonder about the High Priestess herself. He made a mental note to delve deeper into his investigation, determined to uncover the truth behind her extraordinary abilities. But for now, duty called. Lieutenant Pope understood the gravity of his responsibilities as the fleet's sole Laser Fire Control officer. With renewed determination, he prepared to resume his duties, ready to face whatever challenges the Galaxy had in store. As Star Ship 35 set course for its next destination, Lieutenant Pope couldn't help but anticipate the adventures ahead.

Chapter 4

Upon our return to our home station and the docking at Space Station 50, I received a summons to the Captain's day room. Stepping in, The Admiral welcomed me, instantly emphasizing the seriousness of the situation with her presence. She gestured for me to take a seat, her expression hinting at the importance of our impending conversation. It quickly became apparent that significant matters were at hand. The Admiral wasted no time expressing her intention to request a citation for both the troopers and me, acknowledging our exceptional performance during the recent mission.

Furthermore, the Admiral shared news of an upcoming visit from Doctor Ghad, the esteemed mind behind our laser control system. His arrival was to do system upgrades, a prospect that filled me with a sense of responsibility. The Admiral entrusted me with accompanying the doctor and providing any necessary assistance during the upgrade process, which I accepted. Expressing my appreciation for the Admiral's support, I assured her of my commitment to ensuring the success of the upgrade endeavor. Promising to assemble my team to accompany the doctor's team throughout the entire process, I would uphold the standard of excellence expected of us.

Returning to my quarters, I sought to sleep in the quiet embrace of familiar surroundings, hoping to find respite from the weight of recent events. Yet, sleep remained elusive as thoughts of our mission and its sacrifices plagued my mind. The memory of the casualties we endured weighed heavily upon me, stirring feelings of doubt and self-reflection.

Questions gnawed at my conscience—had I failed to devise a more effective plan? Could I have prevented such losses? The uncertainties persisted, unwilling to be quieted. Eventually, exhaustion claimed me, and I surrendered to a restless slumber, knowing that the answers to my questions would have to wait another day.

Doctor Ghad and his team of engineers arrived the following day, and I had the opportunity to introduce myself and my two technicians. "We will accompany you during the upgrade to the laser systems." Glad to meet you, Lieutenant Pope. You are the main reason I'm here doing this upgrade. You destroyed three Reton ships and one Raider without negatively impacting your mental state. Because of mental damage to previous laser control officers, the fleet is no longer installing lasers in their new ships. However, for any ships that still have the lasers and you could become a laser control officer assigned, the fleet has entrusted me with the task of upgrading the systems to enhance their range and control capabilities." It's intriguing, but I have a few inquiries if you don't mind. Certainly, Lieutenant, feel free to ask away. Why hasn't the system been automated yet? Each time the Control system underwent an upgrade to automate the laser fire control, it failed due to the enemy's ability to counteract and destroy the controls during the initial laser shot.". "Moving on to my second question, "How long has this conflict with Roton been ongoing? I've gathered that it seems to have persisted for approximately 500 years.

Additionally, does the empire possess knowledge of the enemy's home system? Surprisingly, the empire hasn't attempted to trace their origins through the wormhole they use to enter our galaxy, per the Empress's orders. She wishes to prevent this situation from escalating into a full-scale war." I thought sooner or later, I would find the location of the Reton home world where I could inflict revenge on them. The doctor and his team have finished the upgrade, and the next step will be to test the systems.

After receiving notification, the Captain was ready to commence the necessary testing following the completion of the upgrade. The vessel received orders to ready itself and locate the specified zone for the laser test. At distances of 6000, 8000, 11,000, and 12,000 yards, system tests confirmed the successful elimination of the simulated enemy ships. The laser system's maximum range was around 8000 yards. The upgrade, however, was anticipated to enhance the range by approximately 20% to 30%. To assess the efficiency of the upgrade. We commenced firing at a simulated target positioned at a distance of 6000 yards. The examination revealed that the hostile vessels were effectively neutralized at ranges of 6000, 8000, 11,000, and 12,000 yards, demonstrating the precision and efficacy of our defensive measures.

Additionally, at 13,000 yards, significant damage was inflicted, further underscoring the effectiveness of our defensive capabilities. The enemy vessel suffered only slight harm from a distance of 14,000 yards. The substantial increase in range would undoubtedly provide us with the advantage of destroying enemy ships before they could even retaliate, leaving me thoroughly impressed with the new firing systems. I eagerly anticipate encountering the Reton Bug heads and defeating them in our upcoming encounters.

As we arrived at station 50 to return the doctor and his team, a sudden commotion seized our attention. The Admiral, accompanied by a squad of approximately 15 troopers, swiftly boarded our vessel. Captain Alara promptly addressed the entire crew via the ship's intercom, disclosing our destination: planet Cothorix station 55. She informed us that the station was currently under assault by the Rotons and urgently requested our assistance. Flanked by two destroyers, our Light cruiser would lead our battle group to station 55. Captain Alara stressed the importance of readiness and urged everyone to prepare for battle stations upon arrival. While it is regrettable that such an attack has occurred, I cannot deny the opportunity it presents. Determined to avenge the harm inflicted upon my home world by the Rotons, I am determined to take every opportunity to remove additional foes. I attended a critical meeting regarding our approach to Station 55. The Admiral wasted no time outlining his strategy. With the participants assembled and anticipation in the air, the Admiral unveiled his plan: deploying two destroyers for initial engagement with the enemy vessels, followed swiftly by the maneuver of the light cruiser. In a strategic move, Lieutenant Pope would take charge of the laser system, neutralizing any remaining adversaries and ensuring the cruiser's safety. The Admiral took a firm and inclusive stance, encouraging everyone to share their perspectives and creating a safe space for open discussions on any concerns. Lifting my hand earned a disapproving glance from my Captain, signaling potential consequences for questioning the Admiral's plan.

Nevertheless, I persisted, giving my perspective on leveraging the extended range of our laser systems for a more effective strategy. I proposed positioning the cruiser at the forefront, catching the enemy off guard from a distance of 13,000 meters, while strategically placing the destroyers at the wormhole entrance to intercept reinforcements and cut off escape routes for the enemy vessels. The Admiral took a moment to consider my proposal before his expression softened into a smile, indicating his approval. He invited further input, but none was forthcoming. With the Admiral recognizing the validity of my plan, he agreed to adopt the adjusted strategy. The crew was assigned to prepare for the imminent battle, and the meeting ended with a dismissal. After the meeting, as we traveled through the wormhole, Anticipation filled my thoughts, and I pondered the success of my plan. The weight of potential complications loomed over me, reminding me of the consequences awaited if my plan failed.

As we exited from the wormhole, I entered the laser control Pode. I assumed my duties of inspecting the system for its flawless operation. After completing a thorough check to ensure all systems functioned correctly, I donned the targeting view helmet. To my surprise, I immediately noticed five enemy ships attacking Station 55. As we closed in at a distance of 13,000 meters, I observed the enemy ships remained unaware of our approach as they were fully engrossed in their assault on the station. As soon as the opportunity presented itself, I fired a concentrated beam of a fiery yellow laser at the first vessel, causing it to explode in a brilliant flash. Without wasting time, I swiftly shifted my aim to the second vessel and unleashed another mighty blast of laser fire, obliterating it into nothingness. However, before I could turn my sights to the third vessel, its sensors must have detected our presence, and it retaliated by launching a missile directly at us. Acting quickly, I aimed and fired at the incoming threat, successfully destroying it before it could reach us. Without hesitation, I directed all my energy toward the third vessel and watched with satisfaction as it met its doom.

But the battle was far from over. The fourth vessel began unleashing a barrage of two missiles in our direction. With expert precision, I intercepted and destroyed them both before they could do any damage. And then, with one final blast of my laser beam, I took out the fourth vessel in a spectacular explosion.

Meanwhile, the fifth vessel seemed to realize their futile efforts and strategically retreated toward the wormhole exit. The Roten ship did not know that destroyers were waiting for them at the entrance to the wormhole. I refrained from pursuing it and instead focused on securing the area around Station 55.

After ensuring no more immediate threats, I took a moment to catch my breath and assess the situation. We had emerged victorious against five powerful enemy vessels thanks to my quick thinking and precise actions. It was just another day defending our territory in battle with the Rotons.

At this point, I had finished my duty at the laser fire control system and decided to exit the pod. The Captain welcomed me with praise for a job well done. Soon after, the station notified us that a shuttle from an enemy ship had landed and released a team of highly trained fighters. In reaction, the Captain promptly ordered the troopers to head to the shuttle Bay and prepare to travel to the station. They aimed to confront and overcome the enemy soldiers infiltrating the station. Quietly and discreetly, I went to my quarters to retrieve my M35 rifle and flack jacket. Upon my arrival at the shuttle bay, I immediately noticed that the troopers had already boarded the shuttle. As I entered, the major welcomed me back on board. The shuttle bay door closed swiftly without delay, and we began our journey towards the station. Taking advantage of the moment, the Major asked me about my previous encounters with the formidable Reton aliens, seeking any advice I could provide. Confidently, I shared my knowledge, explaining that these aliens had a protective yellow shell covering their entire bodies, making them impervious to laser and projectile attacks. However, revealed their weakness was their head, specifically their four eyes. I stressed targeting their head was the only effective way to defeat them, based on my successful experiences.

On our arrival in the shuttle bay, we executed a rapid strategy, swiftly deploying from both sides of the shuttle. Positioned on the right side, the Lieutenant of the troopers and their team found themselves immediately engaged in hostile fire from the Rotons, resulting in the unfortunate injury of two troopers in quick succession. Meanwhile, the Major and I exited from the vessel's left side to assess the situation. With precision, I targeted one of the Rotons directly in its vulnerable head, effectively killing it in a single, decisive strike. Simultaneously, the Major expertly unleashed a lethal shot, swiftly dispatching the second Roton before it could pose a further threat. Recognizing the critical nature of the situation, we wasted no time securing the injured troopers, so we loaded the casualties onto the shuttle, ensuring their swift evacuation for urgent medical attention aboard the cruiser. We communicated with the pilot, issuing clear instructions for immediately transporting the injured troopers back to the cruiser's medical facilities for urgent treatment. Furthermore, the importance of the pilot's prompt return to the station emphasizes the need for swift action to mitigate any potential further threats and ensure the safety and security of all personnel involved in the mission.

We encountered a distressing scene as we ventured into the shuttle Bay. Two members of the service station security were lifeless, while a third was severely injured. The injured security personnel revealed to us there were two additional Rotons on the level above in the cafeteria section of the maintenance department. Furthermore, he informed us that the Baroness had instructed the security team to escort her two daughters back to the planet for their safety. However, the Rotons unexpectedly obstructed our path to the shuttle Bay, and we found ourselves under fire. Unfortunately, the two daughters have been taken and are now being kept captive in the cafeteria with the two aggressive Rotons. The station has taken precautions by sealing off all access to the upper levels, posing a significant challenge for us. Realizing the gravity of the situation, I turned to the major and expressed my concern about the delicate task of neutralizing Rotons without harming the hostages. She acknowledged the severity of the issue and agreed extreme caution would be necessary.

While heading towards the cafeteria, we unexpectedly encountered gunfire from the two Rotons behind the cafeteria's extensive refrigeration system. To protect ourselves from laser fire, we quickly flipped over several Metal tables to serve as makeshift shields. Realizing the gravity of the situation, we knew we had to retaliate, but we had to be cautious, as any stray shots could harm the two hostages. Sadly, we found ourselves constrained by the fact that explosive devices and excessive firepower were not feasible alternatives for us. Despite these constraints, we went over various tactics to rescue the hostages. Ultimately, the Major decided she and one of the troopers would attempt to advance toward a counter section on the left side of the cafeteria. This vantage point would give them a better sight of where the Rotons hid. I expressed my concerns about her vulnerability to enemy fire during the dash to the section. She firmly believed there was no other alternative, and we had to proceed with this course.

The Major and her trooper companion ran towards cover behind a countertop, dodging laser beams from the Toton creatures. Without warning, a barrage of red lasers rained down on the trooper, ripping through her body and sending her crashing to the ground. The Major managed to crawl to safety behind a table despite being struck in the leg. Realizing that she needed help, I made the risky decision to crawl out to her, asking the trooper lieutenant to provide cover fire while keeping an eye on the hostages and holding off the enemy. Inch by inch, I made my way towards the wounded Major, who was still conscious but in serious condition. She refused to leave without retrieving her fallen comrade's body first, but I had to break the news that it was too late. With no other option, I urged her to hold onto my belt as I dragged her back towards safety. The Rotons kept firing at us, but the troopers behind tables provided cover and returned fire.

After a tense and challenging journey, we finally reached safety. Two troopers were immediately assigned to assist the Major back to the shuttle for medical attention aboard the cruiser.

As the Major's attempt to free the hostages failed, I quickly assessed the situation and searched for an alternative route. My eyes landed on a metal ventilation duct, elevated and leading directly above the Rotons' location in the cafeteria. Without hesitation, I handed my M35 rifle to the Lieutenant, instructing her to keep the bug heads occupied while being careful not to harm any of the hostages. She questioned how I would disable the bulkheads without my weapon, but I assured her I had one. With their help, The troopers lifted me onto the veneration duck work, and I crawled to the Roton's location. The ancient weapons given to me by the high priestess materialized in my right hand. Positioned directly above the bug heads, I aimed and fired at both of them, targeting their vulnerable heads. As they fell dead to the ground, I signaled the Lieutenant that the danger had passed. She immediately sprang into action, freeing the frightened hostages huddled in a corner of the room. With everyone safely evacuated from the area, we regrouped and debriefed on our success. Then, I revealed my hidden arsenal and explained how it had helped us in our mission. Grateful and relieved, we returned to Starshipp 136, knowing we had completed another dangerous mission against our alien enemies.

The two daughters of the Baroness thanked us for saving them for the Rotons. A Shulte from the planet arrived at the station with the Baroness just before we were ready to return to the ship. She greeted us as heroes for saving her daughters. She said she was indebted to us, and if we ever needed anything, we should contact her. Everyone was in good humor as we departed for the ship.

Back on the Cruser, the following occurred as the mission progressed: the Captain and Admiral closely monitored the station cameras, their eyes fixed on the live feed. The Admiral turned towards the Captain, a mix of surprise and concern evident on her face. "Did I just see Pope leave the shuttle?" she asked, seeking confirmation. The Captain nodded, her expression grave. "Yes, and he was explicitly instructed not to disembark with the troopers anymore." The Admiral shook her head in disbelief, frustration creeping into her voice. Just then, a signal came from the station reporting that Lieutenant Pope and the troopers had defeated the insurgents and rescued the Baroness's daughters. The Captain was still seething. "It's reckless! He seems to engage in dangerous activities without a second thought." Her tone turned serious as she contemplated the consequences. "He's going to face charges for disobeying a direct order, no doubt." The Admiral's response carried a hint of caution. While the statement remains valid, it is essential to acknowledge the possible political implications that may arise. Pope has rescued the Baroness's daughters and secured the entire station. Letting him off might be in the best interest of the fleet's reputation, especially since the news networks also have access to the station cameras."

A communication arrived, bearing the seal of the Empress herself. Upon receiving the message, the Admiral, a figure of authority and respect, wasted no time. With a solemn demeanor, he began to read the words aloud, each syllable resounding in the chamber." Upon your return home," he intoned, his voice carrying the weight of the Empress's decree, "a commendation ceremony awaits to honor the exceptional courage and dedication displayed by your group in the successful rescue of Station 55 and its hostages. Congratulations on a mission executed with utmost skill and bravery!" The words hung in the air, punctuated by the moment's significance. The message, bearing the official signature of Emperes Cyess, carried the weight of imperial authority, leaving no room for doubt or hesitation. With this confirmation, any lingering uncertainties regarding political correctness evaporated. Standing alongside the Admiral, the Captain nodded in agreement, silently acknowledging the gravity of their achievement and the recognition bestowed upon their efforts.

When I returned to the ship, I received instructions to proceed to the Captain's office. As I stepped inside, the tense atmosphere was palpable, and it was evident from the Captain's expression that she was far from pleased with me. With a stern tone, she wasted no time reprimanding me for my actions and the apparent disobedience of a direct order. Despite the gravity of her words, she mentioned that, owing to the sensitive political circumstances, the consequences would only be a reprimand on my record. After the somewhat sobering meeting with the Captain, I proceeded to the medical section with a mix of apprehension. There, I found hope in the sight of the Major, who, against the odds, was conscious and greeted me with genuine warmth. "I'm glad you're still alive," she said. "I owe you a great deal for saving me." In response, I nodded, conveying that it was an honor to have assisted. After all, in our ranks, loyalty and solidarity were unwavering principles, and leaving a comrade behind was never an option. Before leaving the medical section, I made it a point to personally check on the well-being of the other troopers, ensuring that their road to recovery was progressing positively. It was a small gesture that perhaps echoed the profound sense of camaraderie that defined our unit—a reminder that we stood together in the face of adversity, steadfast and unwavering.

As I returned to my quarters, a sense of satisfaction washed over me, surpassing even my highest expectations. The outcome of our mission had unfolded remarkably well, exceeding every hope I had harbored. Moreover, our successful retaliation against the Rotons for their brazen assault on Station 55 filled me with a fierce sense of determination. Eagerly, I anticipated the opportunity to inflict even more significant harm upon them, ensuring they faced the full consequences of their actions. I am resolute in pursuing them tirelessly, ensuring justice and the Empire remains secure from potential harm.

Chapter 5

When we reached station 55, the Empress had organized an elaborate military ceremony to greet us, instilling a feeling of honor and gratitude. The purpose of this ceremony was to pay tribute to the efforts undertaken by our group during the rescue mission of Station 55 and its hostages. It was an incredibly proud and honorable moment for all of us. The ceremony took place in the magnificent courtyard of the Imperial Palace. As we stood in formation, awaiting the ceremony's commencement, the Empress took the stage. Her words deeply showed appreciation for our accomplishments and sacrifices in the name of duty.

The Empress addressed the crowd with a commanding voice, conveying a sense of authority as she recounted the unfolding events at Station 55. She spoke of the intense siege that had taken place, highlighting the remarkable bravery displayed by our forces. With great pride, she emphasized the ultimate success of the daring rescue mission,

During the ceremony, as it progressed with solemn dignity, Admael Astra, Captain Alara, and I stood at the forefront of the assembly, anticipation, and reverence as we awaited the forthcoming announcement from the Empress. Then, in a resonant voice that commanded attention, the Empress declared the awarding of the Medal of Mattoris Service to all officers and fleet personnel present—an emblem of exceptional dedication and sacrifice in service to the empire. It was a moment of collective recognition, a testament to the courage and commitment of every individual within the ranks.

Furthermore, Ademel Astrs, Captain Alara, and I were honored with the Metal of Gallantry in the face of the empire's enamines for their unwavering dedication to defending the empire. The Emperess awarded me the Star Of Empire, a metal awarded only four times, for his heroic actions at station 55, which saved numerous lives. She also promoted me to lieutenant commander, and he will be transferred to the empress guard and available to the fleet when needed. Yet, amidst the swell of commendation and honor, a solemn acknowledgment lingered—a poignant reminder of those who had made the ultimate sacrifice. We bowed our heads in a moment of silent tribute to the brave troopers who had fallen in the line of duty, their deeds forever etched in the annals of our collective memory.

As the ceremony drew to a close, my thoughts drifted to the faces of those around me—their expressions of pride and quiet contemplation. At that moment, amidst the echoes of praise and remembrance, I grappled with a tumult of emotions. How had I come to stand here amidst such esteemed company, and what lay ahead in my chosen path? It was a question that lingered, unanswered yet with possibility, as I contemplated the journey that had brought me to this pivotal moment. I am the only male in this situation amidst a sea of females. The uncertainty of what lies ahead in my future looms over me, making it impossible to predict what awaits me.

Following the ceremony, the Empress invited all officers and the Ship's crew to gather in the Great Hall and personally greet the Empress. During the event, the Admiral took the opportunity to introduce me to my new commanding officer, Captain Xela. She told me she would discuss my responsibilities when I reported for duty the following day. Furthermore, she assured me she would introduce me to the Empress upon arriving. Curious about the appropriate etiquette, I Inquired whether I should bow or kneel when presented to her. With a warm smile, my commanding officer reassured me there was no need for such formalities and advised me to allow the Empress to initiate the conversation.

As the Empress and her companion entered the room, a wave of respect and admiration swept through the crowd, prompting everyone to rise and extend warm greetings. Expressing her gratitude for their presence, the Empress conveyed her hope everyone had found joy in the ceremony. I discovered that her companion was her daughter, Princess Lasre, who radiated elegance as a respected member of the royal household. It was Captain Xela who introduced me to the Empress. At that moment, she conveyed her appreciation, stating, "The empire is indebted to you for your valiant efforts in safeguarding station 55 from the Roton's attack. Your assignment to the guard is a testament to the empire's recognition of your service.", I expressed thanks to her and the empire for everything they had done for me.

After leaving their presence, the Princess joined me, showing a surprising depth of knowledge about my encounters with Retons, gleaned from both my written records and the videos. Her genuine interest in my experiences prompted her to ask, "How are you managing the many changes in your life?" I responded," Adapting to professional changes is a part of life. One must handle them as they arise." After our conversation, the Princess departed. Her thoughtful inquiries lingered in my mind, leading me to ponder the underlying motive behind our conversation. Could she have a genuine interest in me beyond mere curiosity about my adventures? Yet, I cautioned myself against allowing my ego to seize control of my thoughts, acknowledging my origins devoid of royal lineage or with the ruling families of the Empire planets might render such speculation unfounded. The remainder of the evening unfolded in camaraderie and laughter as I enjoyed the warmth of my friend's company. With a reassuring smile during the celebration,

Captain Xela, the security head, approached me and notified me that she had relocated items to an apartment on the palace grounds. The way she spoke showed both warmth and efficiency, assuring me of a smooth transition into my new position within the empire's service. As the night wore on and the festivities began to wane, Captain Xela graciously offered to accompany me back to my new room, a gesture of kindness that spoke volumes about her leadership and concern for those under her command. With her by my side, I navigated the winding corridors of the palace. Upon stepping into my new quarters, To my surprise, the view I encountered surpassed all my expectations. The apartment had a remarkably snug atmosphere, a spacious living area with sophisticated furnishings, a wall-mounted screen, and a small yet efficient kitchenette. Moving further into the apartment, I discovered a bedroom featuring a queen-sized bed, its linens a testament to the attention to detail that permeated every corner of the space. I was pleased to find that all my possessions from the Starship were present, making my new environment feel familiar and welcoming. As I surveyed the scene before me, a sense of gratitude washed over me, mingled with a tinge of disbelief at the generosity of the accommodations provided. Moreover, the sight of my storage container nestled within the confines of a spacious walk-in closet filled me with a sense of reassurance, knowing that everything I needed was within arm's reach. With a sigh, I resolved to meet with Captain Xela the following day to discuss my upcoming assignments, eager to embark on this new chapter of my journey within the empire's service. As I settled into the comfort of my new home, anticipation mingled with a sense of purpose and anticipation for the challenges and adventures ahead.

To my astonishment, I received an unexpected opportunity the next day: an invitation to attend a commendation ceremony on the Trooper's planet. I was permitted to participate by the guard commander. Grateful for the honor bestowed upon me, I eagerly accepted the chance to partake in this occasion. Boarding the shuttle bound for the space station, I couldn't shake the anticipation as I embarked on this journey to a world imbued with the courage and resilience of the troopers.

Upon my arrival, I met the imposing figure of General Nely, whose reputation preceded her as a stalwart defender of the empire's borders. Her demeanor exuded a blend of authority and warmth as she extended her gratitude for my contributions during the harrowing assault on Station 55 and my steadfast support in aiding the troopers in achieving their objectives. In a gesture that surprised me, General Nely revealed plans for a forthcoming ceremony where I would be decorated and elevated to honorary major. The revelation left me momentarily speechless, grappling with the weight of this unexpected promotion in light of my current position as a commander within the fleet. However, General Nely reassured me the Empress herself had sanctioned this honor, instilling a newfound sense of pride and responsibility within me.

I steeled myself for the challenges ahead, knowing that I carried the weight of my achievements and the expectations of those who had trusted me. I stood among the troopers with a mixture of reverence and gratitude. When called upon to address the assembly, I approached the podium with purpose, my words infused with the echoes of camaraderie and shared sacrifice."I am deeply honored to have stood shoulder to shoulder with the brave warriors of the 59th regiment," I began, my voice carrying across the sea of faces assembled before me. "In the face of adversity, we have upheld a sacred bond, never wavering in our commitment to one another. For on my home planet, we hold fast to the belief that no comrade shall ever be left behind, whether fallen or standing. It is a creed that binds us together in unity and strength, guiding our actions on the battlefield and beyond." As I spoke, I could feel the collective spirit of the troopers resonating with my words, a testament to the indomitable resolve that defined our shared journey. At that moment, amidst the applause and camaraderie, I knew I stood not as an individual but as a part of something greater. As I looked upon the faces of those gathered before me, I knew we would face whatever the future held, bound by the unbreakable bonds of loyalty and courage. I hope the 59th regiment can adopt the same ethos."A wave of applause erupted from the troopers, their approval palpable. In the moment, I couldn't help but acknowledge the exceptional caliber of these soldiers, among the finest I had ever fought alongside. As the ceremony drew to a close, General Nely extended her gratitude once more and invited me to an after-ceremony gathering where I had the opportunity to mingle with the officers of the 59th regiment. Surrounded by camaraderie and mutual respect, the event proved to be a memorable and enjoyable affair, a testament to the bonds forged in the heat of battle.

I met with the palace guard on my return from the Trooper's plant. The Captain notified me that The automated Taylor would send my new work attire and dress uniforms from the administration office to my apartment. They had already obtained all my clothing measurements from the fleet, ensuring a perfect fit. Moreover, I received my new ID card, which officially identified me as a member of the Palace Guard personnel. The financial officer approached me and requested instructions on where to allocate my well-deserved bonuses. To my surprise, I had been awarded 135,000 credits for successfully destroying four Reton ships and received an unexpected amount of 500,000 for earning the prestigious Star of the Empire medal. This news completely caught me off guard, leaving me momentarily speechless. After careful consideration, I donated a portion of my bonus to the Church of Faith as a charitable contribution. It felt like the right thing to do, as I wanted to give back to the church for treating my wounds and the gift by the high priestess of the ancient laser weapon. The remaining bonus amount would be deposited into my debit account, allowing me to save and manage my finances effectively.

It was a moment of gratitude and responsibility as I realized the impact of my achievements and the opportunities they presented.

As part of my new role, I accompanied the palace captain on a tour to familiarize myself with the various responsibilities. During the tour, we explored the extensive camera systems installed throughout the palace, which provided surveillance coverage of almost every area except the living quarters. They told me I would have access to the camera monitoring system, allowing me to observe all activities within the palace. She emphasized my primary duty would be to attend and ensure the safety of the Empress and her guests during all significant events. Curious about potential threats, I inquired about the Empress's safety concerns. The Captain responded affirmatively, mentioning powerful political groups who might attempt to replace her with a mere figurehead. Determined to fulfill my responsibilities diligently, I assured the Captain I would prevent harm from befalling the Empress under my watch. Relieved to hear my commitment, I expressed my readiness to begin my duties promptly.

However, the Captain informed me that, according to fleet policy, I would not commence immediately. Instead, I am scheduled for Rejuvenation treatment in two days, questioning the necessity of undergoing this treatment. She explained it was a mandatory procedure enforced by the fleet policy. Although initially taken aback, I accepted the requirement with some fear because my DNA was not a perfect match for this society. Let's hope I come through this ok. A few days later, I find myself standing at the rejuvenation center, anticipation beneath the surface as I prepare for what comes next.

Before the commencement of the procedure, I pause to address a series of pressing questions that have been weighing on my mind. "Doctor, my DNA is only a 93 percent match," I begin, my voice tinged with a hint of apprehension, "could this potentially pose a problem?" The doctor meets my inquiry with a reassuring smile and a demeanor of professionalism and empathy. With precision, he explains that the rejuvenation treatment operates on a cellular level, targeting and enhancing the body's natural repair and regeneration mechanisms. "Your DNA match is not a direct concern," he assures me. His words help to ease my anxieties. "The treatment focuses on optimizing cellular function, irrespective of genetic variations." At this point, he gave me the following article to read.

DEVELOPED BY LEADING scientists 500 years ago, the rejuvenation process extends human life by 100 years and paves the way for a second rejuvenation, doubling lifespan to a remarkable 200 years.

1. ***Cellular Rejuvenation*** *is a state-of-the-art nanotechnology in the form of CRNs. These tiny, specialized nanobots are programmed to target and repair damaged cells throughout the body at the molecular level. CRNs reverse aging by rejuvenating cells and restoring youthful vitality and function.*

2. ***Genetic Restoration Therapy (GRT):*** *In conjunction with incorporates advanced Genetic Restoration Therapy. GRT works by identifying and repairing genetic mutations and damage accumulating over time, leading to a decline in aging. By restoring the integrity of DNA, GRT ensures that cells function optimally, promoting longevity and vitality.*

3. ***Organ Regeneration Matrix (ORM):*** *To complement cellular Rejuvenation, employ an Organ Regeneration Matrix. This innovative system stimulates the body's natural regenerative capabilities, prompting the repair and regeneration of aging organs and tissues. ORM ensures that vital organs maintain optimal function, enhancing overall health and longevity.*

4. ***Biofeedback Integration Interface (BII):*** *Central to the process*

is the Biofeedback Integration Interface. This sophisticated system continuously monitors and analyzes the body's physiological parameters. By providing personalized feedback and adjustments, BII ensures that the rejuvenation process is tailored to each individual, maximizing effectiveness and safety.

5. ***Rejuvenation Reiteration Protocol (RRP):*** *Perhaps the most revolutionary aspect of Rejuvenation Reiteration Protocol is a feature that allows individuals to undergo a second rejuvenation process, extending their lifespan by 100 years. By combining the latest advancements in biotechnology and medical science, RRP offers the promise of a lifespan unprecedented in human history.*

As the doctor elaborates on the intricacies of the procedure, I find myself absorbing each detail with a growing sense of understanding and reassurance. My age difference should not affect the procedure's effectiveness. "Your biological age may differ," he acknowledges, "but the underlying principles of cellular rejuvenation remain steadfast." With a sense of relief washing over me like a tide, I nod in acknowledgment. "Alright then, let's proceed.

The doctor nods in response, his expression a testament to his commitment to ensuring a seamless and comfortable experience. "Rest assured," he assures me, "you will be asleep throughout the process, allowing for a tranquil and undisturbed rejuvenation."

Upon awakening from the treatment, I immediately noticed the medical staff seemed to be constantly peering into my room. Curiosity got the better of me, so when the doctor finally entered, I couldn't help but inquire about the reason behind their constant surveillance. Worriedly, I asked, "Is there something wrong with me? People keep looking in at me." To my relief, the doctor reassured me, "No need to worry. All your vital signs are perfectly normal. However, there is one remarkable difference in your case." he handed me a mirror. As I gazed into it, I couldn't believe my eyes. "Good lord, I look ten years younger!" The doctor calmly explained, "Indeed, most patients tend to appear slightly younger after the treatment, but the transformation is more pronounced in your case.

Nevertheless, it poses no problem. Just rest, and we will discharge you in the morning." I was grateful for the doctor's explanation, expressed my gratitude, and eagerly awaited my departure from the hospital. As I returned from the rejuvenation process, I settled back into my duties at the palace.

Back at the castle, the Captain relayed the news of an upcoming formal event where I would be honored to accompany one of the Baronesses, Elysia, and her daughter. Curiosity piqued, I inquired about the nature of my role as an escort. The Captain assured me my sole responsibility would be to accompany her to the event, leaving any additional activities at my discretion. He emphasized I had the freedom to decline any requests she might make as long as I did so with utmost politeness.

As I navigated through the event that evening, I felt uneasy due to my lack of familiarity with the proper etiquette and protocol expected of me. I finally reached the reception area to meet the Baroness and her daughter in a full dress uniform adorned with medals. To my surprise, the Baroness greeted me with a warm smile and a playful comment about the unusual presence of a male escort by her side. Her friendly demeanor and the way she addressed me by name, referring to me as Commander Pope, immediately put me at ease and piqued my curiosity about the upcoming events of the evening. The Baroness and her daughter were engaged in a pleasant and casual conversation with me, creating a light and enjoyable atmosphere. Entering the grand hall, the announcer highlighted our presence, emphasizing the Baroness's title as ruler of a distant planet and my own as the holder of the prestigious Star of the Empire. After exchanging pleasantries with the Empress, we were escorted to our designated table, marking the beginning of what promised to be an intriguing and memorable evening and fascinating conversations. The unexpected turn of events and the warm reception from the Baroness and the Empress left me eager to see what the rest of the night had in store.

I enjoyed a delightful dinner with the Barness and engaged in a pleasant conversation. As dinner came to a close, after our meal, the Baroness approached her daughter and suggested that she and the commander take a stroll in the emperor's garden, which was a truly stunning place to visit. I couldn't resist the offer, so we both stood up from the table and went to the garden, engaging in a delightful conversation. "Well, commander, you've made quite an impression on my mother. Otherwise, she wouldn't have invited us to explore the garden together. I believe she's hoping to find me a suitable partner," she said with a smile. Unsure of how to respond, I smiled back at her. She turned to me and continued, "Don't be so surprised, commander. My mother is always trying to find a match for me." "Let's just inform her that we had a pleasant conversation, and perhaps in the future, there might be an opportunity for us to meet again," she suggested. With that, I took the hand of this enchanting woman, and together, we made our way back to the ball.

While seated at the table, I reflected on my decision years ago regarding my personal life. As a combat veteran, I made a conscious choice not to pursue long-term relationships with the opposite sex due to the inherent dangers of my profession. The thought of putting a wife and family through the anguish of my potential demise on a mission weighed heavily on my conscience, leading me to believe it would be unkind to subject them to such uncertainty. Despite my resolve, I do find solace in brief interactions with the opposite sex. However, I acknowledge the challenge of maintaining boundaries when faced with individuals who are captivating and seemingly perfect in every way. The internal conflict between my principles and desires is a constant struggle that I grapple with, unsure of the right path to take in such situations.

As the realization struck me, I did not know what this event was for. To shed light on the purpose of the gathering, I approach Baroness, hoping for some clarity."Excuse me," I ventured, with a hint of uncertainty, "but could you kindly enlighten me about the significance of this event?" To my astonishment, Barness turned to me with a knowing smile as if anticipating my question. "Ah, allow me to elucidate," she began. "We have convened here to witness a pivotal moment in our empire's history: the transition of power. Empress Cyess, after years of illustrious reign, is gracefully stepping down from her throne, paving the way for her daughter Lasra to ascend as the new leader of our vast empire."

BARONESSES ARE HEREDITARY rulers of the human planets, situated within a star system,

1. ***Cultural Diversity and Adaptation:***
   - *Each planet within the empire has its unique culture, history, and environmental conditions. Baronesses must adapt their governance style to suit each planet's population's particular needs and nuances.*

2. ***Technological Advancement and Resource Management:***
   - *The empire invests heavily in technological research and development to ensure efficient resource management, sustainability, and prosperity across all planets.*

3. ***Education and Innovation:***
   - *Education takes precedence in nurturing creativity, analytical thinking, and societal advancement. Baronesses establish comprehensive educational systems tailored to the specific needs of*

each planet, nurturing talent and fostering a culture of lifelong learning.

4. ***Inclusive Governance and Representation:***
   - *Baronesses govern in consultation with councils comprised of representatives from various sectors of society, ensuring inclusivity, transparency, and accountability in decision-making processes.*

5. ***Interplanetary Cooperation and Diplomacy:***
   - *The empire fosters cooperation and mutual benefit among its planets through diplomatic initiatives and trade agreements.*

6. ***Empress as Guardian of the Realm:***
   - *The Empress serves as the ultimate authority, ensuring the integrity of the empire's governance and the well-being of its citizens.*
   - *While Baronesses wield significant autonomy, the Empress safeguards against tyranny or neglect, intervening if a Baroness fails to uphold the empire's values or fulfill her responsibilities to her people.*

THE GRAND PLATFORM was already bustling with activity as the Empress and Princess made their way to take their place. Standing guard nearby, I always remained alert, scanning the sea of eager dignitaries awaiting the upcoming announcement. But something caught my eye in the crowd - two servers exchanging furtive signals as they maneuvered closer to the stage. My keen senses detected a glimmer of steel concealed within one of their hands, and without hesitation, I sprang into action. The grand platform buzzed with anticipation as the Empress and Princess strode forward, regal and composed. As their loyal guard, I kept a sharp eye on the bustling crowd of dignitaries, scanning for potential threats. Suddenly, my keen senses picked up on two servers exchanging furtive signals amidst the sea of people. My trained eyes caught a glint of metal hidden in one of their hands, and my muscles tensed. Without hesitation, I swiftly moved towards them, ready to protect the rulers at all costs.

With a quick flick of my wrist, a laser materialized in my grasp. As I surveyed the room, I saw the first server reaching for something hidden beneath the server's apron - most likely a concealed weapon. Without hesitation, I aimed and fired, the beam of light hitting the server square in the head and bringing her down before she could harm anyone else. My attention then shifted to the second attacker, who had revealed a deadly blade from within her robe. With expert precision, I aimed and fired again, this time striking her in the chest and effectively neutralizing the threat. The room fell silent as both assailants lay lifeless on the floor, their hostile intentions thwarted. Despite the tension and murmurs that began to rise in the room, I remained vigilant and ready for any further threats that may arise in this volatile political climate.

The Empress and Princess were furious with me, their voices echoing as they exclaimed, "Are you out of your mind? You just shot and killed two of our servants!" However, before the situation could escalate further, the Captain stepped forward and addressed the room. He calmly reassured everyone, saying, "It's alright; these individuals I identified as assassins by the intricate tattoos adorning their skin." The commander's swift actions had successfully put an end to the assassination attempt.

Overwhelmed with relief, the Princess rushed towards me and embraced me tightly. Grateful, she whispered, "You saved both my mother and me from this horrifying act. During the examination of the corpses, the captain advised us not to touch the blades that were scattered on the ground because they might be covered with poison. The astonishing disclosure left everyone in disbelief. " Please, everyone, take your seats while I call in the Empire investigation team. Thank you." The inspector immediately directed them to a nearby room, where the specialized Empire investigation unit would keep them secure for investigation.

The lead investigator inquired about my knowledge of the assassins during the investigation. I explained that two servers were exchanging signals while approaching the platform. One of them caught my attention as she had a concealed blade. She mentioned that she needed my laser as per regulations, to which I expressed doubt. I raised my arm to prove my point, and the laser materialized. I challenged her to try and take it, but the laser vanished as soon as she touched it. I then recounted the laser's origin, a gift from the High Priestess. "I acknowledge and appreciate your explanation. Thank you for your prompt response to the situation. This entire incident had the potential to plunge the empire into chaos, with various factions vying for power. Your actions have truly served the empire well."

Following the conclusion of the investigation, all individuals were permitted to depart. I located the Baroness and accompanied her to her quarters within the castle's confines. She expressed concern for my well-being in the aftermath of the killing of the two assassins. I reassured her I would be alright; such occurrences were not uncommon in my work, and one learns to adapt to such situations over time. Curious about an assassin guild within a society boasting advanced technological capabilities, I wondered why the empire permitted such an organization to operate. The Baroness explained the guild had been a longstanding institution for millennia, much like the tradition of passing down the title of Empress to female heirs. She emphasized this acceptance was deeply ingrained in the fabric of society, leaving me trying to understand such a system. I bid her good night and returned to my post.

Chapter 6

At my duty station, I received a call to attend a meeting about an unknown subject. When I entered the room, I saw Ademal Astra, two other admirals, and the Empress and her daughter were already seated. The Empress initiated the discussion by stating the urgent need for a plan to counter the empire's problem with the Rotens. She specifically requested our input. One of the admirals, whom we had not previously met, immediately proposed increasing the number of fleet ships patrolling the border to gain advanced warning of Roton's actions. However, he also acknowledged the high cost of this plan, which the empire would have to bear if it resulted in saved lives. She then turned to Ademal Astra and asked for her agreement with the plan, emphasizing she would be responsible for selecting the manufacturer and determining the number of new ships. "it sounds like a good plan; I will proceed as director."

She turned to me. "Commander Pope, do you have anything to say about the plan"? Feeling the weight of the situation, I recalled a previous meeting with Ademal Astra, where she had warned me to be cautious about my words, as both the other admirals expressed concerns about the negative impact of my prominent position as the only male officer in the fleet. They had even hinted at the possibility of removing me from service at that moment. I contemplated whether I should conform to the suggested plan or present my ideas to tackle the issue with the Rotons effectively. After careful consideration, I decided to voice my opinion, disregarding any potential consequences. "

propose a different approach," I confidently stated, "let us equip a starship with a substantial arsenal of nuclear weaponry and automate its operations. This way, we can strategically target and eliminate the home planet of the Rotons." The Rotons, much like the bees on my father's farm, possess a hierarchical structure with a queen capable of producing abundant workers and warriors as required. However, when a new queen emerges, they seek suitable habitats to accommodate her. This constant search for a new home for their queen poses a perpetual threat. The only viable solution to halt their expansion is to instill a deep fear of annihilation within them.

One of the Ademals pointed out that Commander Pope's suggestion of a suicide mission to commit genocide against the Rotons could potentially ignite an all-out war. The Empress sympathized with my desire for revenge following the devastating attack on my home. However, she expressed her concerns about the empire's decision to engage in genocide. Despite this, she clarified that we would proceed with the Admiral Astra plan. Later, admirals Astra requested my assistance in expanding the fleet ships. The Empress readily agreed, expressing gratitude for their input and promising to start working on the plans promptly. The meeting adjourned, and I returned to my duty station.

Later that week, I received a call from Admiral Astra, who required my assistance reviewing two starship manufacturers. Their selection would be crucial for the empire's defense against the impending Roton invasion. Despite my initial hesitation, I expressed my concerns about lacking engineering expertise. However, the Admiral reassured me, stating he wanted me to visit their manufacturing facilities and have a conversation with the head of each one of the manufacturers. I agreed with the importance of providing valuable feedback to the Admiral. I requested the addresses of both manufacturers so that the review process could begin promptly.

During my visit to the first manufacturer, which specialized in shuttle crafts, I met the head of the company and embarked on a thorough tour of their facility. As we went through the bustling corridors and witnessed the meticulous craftsmanship, it became clear that their expertise lay in small-scale shuttlecraft production. Driven by curiosity, I couldn't resist asking if they were expanding their operation to include the construction of war starships. To my surprise, their response was candid. While they confessed to never delving into such endeavors, they were willing to adapt and expand their facility should they be entrusted with the contract. Grateful for their openness and hospitality, I assured them the Admiral would be in touch to discuss further details once the Admiral had decided. Yet, beneath the surface of diplomatic pleasantries, a seed of doubt took root within me. I couldn't shake the nagging question of feasibility, considering the manufacturer's modest size and their lack of experience in starship construction.

Traveling to the following manufacturer, I was greeted by the owner, Altain, setting the tone for yet another facility tour. However, this time, the scope of the operation was nothing short of impressive. The facility's expanse stretched before me, with my gaze immediately drawn to the imposing figure of a starship in mid-construction. It was a freighter-type ship commissioned by a prominent freight company, hinting at the manufacturer's prowess in handling substantial projects.

Eager to gain information, I posed the same question as before, inquiring about their experience in starship construction for military application. The owner's response was fresh air, marked by honesty and a hint of pride. She revealed a rich history of constructing many vessels, ranging from heavy cruisers to light cruisers and destroyers. However, amidst her candid revelations, she shared the company's current struggles and hinted at the looming possibility of closure. Armed with this newfound understanding, I would relay the information to the Admiral, assuring her that the final decision rested with the Admiral.

Yet, despite my initial reservations, a sense of intrigue and possibility began to take root within me. There was an undeniable allure to this facility, an untapped potential that hinted at the possibility of it being the prime choice for our project.

As the day grew late, the owner suggested we grab dinner at a nearby restaurant, with her offering to cover the bill. I appreciated the gesture but insisted on paying. Over dinner, we engaged in a delightful conversation, getting to know each other more personally. On our way back to the factory, she surprised me by inviting me to her apartment, conveniently located at the top of the facility. Intrigued by the prospect, I contemplated starting a new relationship, something I had previously refrained from due to the uncertainties of my profession and its potential dangers. However, perhaps it is time for a change, so I accepted the invitation.

Upon careful analysis of our findings, the Admiral and I unanimously decided that the second manufacturer would be the optimal choice for the contract. Assuming responsibility, the Admiral entrusted me with notifying the company about their successful bid for the construction contract, including the specific quantity and timeline. I got in touch with the owner about our decision. Deeply appreciative of the opportunity, she conveyed her gratitude and eagerly anticipated an upcoming meeting. Furthermore, she expressed her enthusiasm for the growth of our professional relationship. Considering my involvement with the Admiral's team during the ship construction, I anticipate having regular interactions with her shortly. Nevertheless, I am concerned about whether pursuing a romantic relationship with her is the best decision. Only time will reveal if I am making the right choice.

Admiral told me to meet with the Starship facility to review our contract. The contract included a heavy, light cruiser and six destroyers. The company's owner, Altaira, was presented with the contract and immediately understood its importance. After carefully examining it in her office, she signed off without hesitation. Assuming control, she took charge of arranging the precise ship construction order. Her meticulousness and proactive attitude ensure that everything will operate seamlessly and effectively. In keeping with her carefully crafted plans for the remaining ships, the Empress Light Cruiser has been prioritized as the first ship to be built. As I toured the massive facility, I was drawn to a small, unfinished starship on the factory's bustling floor. The smooth lines and shiny surface of the ship stood in stark contrast to the dull, gray surroundings of the manufacturing plant. Curiosity getting the best of me, I asked Altaria, "What's the deal with this ship?" With a sad look, she replied, "That was Cortana's Starship. A vibrant entertainer who ordered it so she could easily travel between events on different planets, showcasing her incredible talent and bringing joy to countless audiences." The weight of her words hit me as she continued, "Unfortunately, Cortana's life was cut short in a tragic shuttle accident, leaving us all saddened by her loss."

Her family made the decision not to complete the private Starship. As I stood in front of it at the facility, my mind wandered to the possibility of purchasing and finishing it. The sleek metallic exterior glistened under the artificial lights, promising adventure and luxury. My thoughts turned to using it to travel back to Earth, my home planet, and the idea was incredibly tempting. But before making any decisions, we needed to consult with Altaira and agree on completing the ship. Such a decision would require careful consideration and thorough planning. As I gazed up at the massive structure, I couldn't help but feel a twinge of apprehension about the daunting task ahead. It would require significant financial resources and technical expertise that I lacked as a novice in piloting starships. Despite the challenges, the allure of owning and traveling in my own private Starship was too great to resist.

After our meeting, the Admiral asked me to stay and compile a list of questions that needed to be answered. Altaira then invited me to join her for lunch to discuss the intricacies of the project. During our meal, I suggested purchasing the unfinished Starship and returning to my home planet. However, as someone who was not a pilot, I emphasized the need for complete automation in the ship's systems. She proposed incorporating an advanced AI system to handle navigation and maintenance tasks. Later, she invited me to visit her apartment that evening, where we could review the plans in more detail and strengthen our partnership. I accepted and agreed to meet at 7:30 tonight.

As I returned to the Admiral's office within the bustling fleet headquarters, I carefully held onto the questions he had given me during our luncheon. The Admiral's expression was now unreadable as he addressed me, her deep voice conveying curiosity and concern. He brought up a topic that caught me off guard - a personal connection between Altaira and myself that he seemed to have noticed. His tone turned serious as he emphasized the need for discretion in our relationship so as not to cause any embarrassment or controversy within the fleet. I reassured him that I understood the gravity of the situation and promised to handle our relationship with utmost care and secrecy. The Admiral seemed satisfied with my response and informed me of a specific request regarding the heavy cruiser. It was to have a unique suite prepared for the Empress, as this vessel would serve as her primary mode of transportation throughout the empire. I nodded attentively, taking mental note of this important task that needed to be prioritized above all others - even above the production of destroyers and light cruisers. As soon as our meeting concluded, I immediately relayed this crucial information to Altaira.

In addition, the massive heavy and sleek light cruisers were to be outfitted with advanced laser control systems, providing an extra layer of protection for the fleet. As a skilled laser control officer, I oversee these systems. The Admiral was pleased with my strategy and gave me a nod of approval. As I exited the office, I made sure that all preparations were in place to meet the specific needs of the Empress, considering every detail down to the smallest item.

In the evening, at her apartment, I proposed creating a unique living space for the Empress on the heavy cruiser. She reassured me that it wouldn't be a problem, as they already had a design from the previous system and could update it to fit her needs. Then, I mentioned my interest in purchasing the small personal Starship. "I thought you might be interested in this," She said as she handed me the plans. "If you have any questions, we can review them tonight." "That sounds great," she replied. We spent considerable time discussing and designing the layout for the ship's interior, ultimately deciding on the following plan.

Starship Layout:

1. First Deck:

Two Master Bedrooms are on opposite sides of the ship for convenience. Each contains a sleeping area, an attached bathroom with a shower and toilet, and ample storage space.

Two Smaller Bedrooms: Positioned next to the master bedrooms for guests or crew members, They feature compact sleeping quarters, storage cabinets, and shared bathroom facilities.

The Living Area and Dining: Situated in the center of the deck, the living area provides a comfortable space for relaxation and socializing. It includes seating arrangements, entertainment systems, and large view screens for stargazing. The dining area is next to the living area, with a table and seating for meals and gatherings.

Food Processing Section: Located near the dining area for convenience, this section contains facilities for storing, preparing, and cooking food. It includes refrigeration units, food processors, stoves, and other culinary equipment to meet the nutritional needs of the crew during long journeys.

Storage Area: Positioned behind the food processing section, this area offers ample space for provisions, supplies, and equipment for operating the Starship.

Bridge: Located at the front of the upper deck, this serves as the command center of the Starship. It houses control panels, navigation systems, communication devices, and monitoring equipment used to pilot and manage the ship's functions. The bridge also offers a panoramic view through large screens. Plus, there is a pode for the laser targeting system.

2. Lower Deck:

Generator and Laser System: This section on the lower deck contains the power generator that fuels all systems and amenities on board. The laser systems serve as defensive and offensive weapons for protecting against potential threats.

Missiles: Positioned strategically on the lower deck, the missiles and launch tubes ensure the Starship's and its occupants' safety and security.

A satisfied smile spread across my face as she nodded in response to my proposal. Skillfully, I redirected the conversation towards acquiring an advanced AI system to navigate and automate all systems on the Starship I had my eyes set on. The ship's interior was sleek and modern, and this cutting-edge technology would only add to its appeal. However, my excitement was quickly dampened when she warned of the risks involved with this particular AI model. She mentioned something about the empire prohibiting the use of such AIs on starships, as they tended to evolve into their independent entities, potentially causing unforeseen problems. Despite her cautionary words, I couldn't resist the allure of having such advanced technology at my disposal. She advised me to keep its installation a secret from authorities if I chose to go through with it. Fully aware of the potential consequences, I knew it was a risk worth taking for a smooth journey back to my home planet.

As our conversation progressed, I requested a laser control system be installed on the ship, along with the ability to fire two rockets for self-defense. Altraia listened attentively and assured me the installation would not be a problem. Altaria mentioned that there were spare laser control systems sitting idle, remnants from the fleet's decision to discontinue their use due to their harmful effects on the officers who operated them. After thorough discussions with the fleet's technical team and finalizing all necessary details, we decided to take a break and enjoy a delectable dinner together. As we savored each bite of our meal, our relationship grew more substantial and solidified, laying the foundation for a successful partnership in navigating the vastness of space.

After settling back into my duties at the castle, I received a message with news of my next assignment: serving as the fire control officer on the Empress's Starship for an upcoming voyage. The new Empress had expressed a strong desire to personally meet with influential Baronesses from seven key planets within our empire system. It would be an incredible tour, full of opportunities for diplomacy and alliance-building. As the assigned fire control officer, I was responsible for ensuring the safety and security of all passengers and crew during our travels. Though the weight of this duty was heavy, I was determined to excel and contribute to the success of this vital journey. Upon receiving this assignment, I informed Altaira that I would be leaving town for a special mission for the Empress and promised to contact her upon my return. When I reached the space station, I was at the check-in line for the Empress's Starship. The troopers were thorough in their security checks, carefully verifying the IDs of all officers before granting them access to board the ship. Their attention to detail and dedication to their duty ensured the safety and well-being of everyone on board.

As I approached the check-in point, I noticed an interesting detail: the troopers did not salute the officers. It was a long-standing tradition for them only to salute their superiors. But then, unexpectedly, the trooper Lieutenant called the unit to attention, and they all saluted me. I felt uneasy under this sudden attention, especially since the other officers gave me strange looks. Perhaps they remembered my previous encounters with the troopers at Station 55. While I was grateful for recognizing my actions during the combat mission, I couldn't help but worry about how my fellow command staff would perceive them. As the only male officer in the fleet, I knew this particular treatment could cause tension and resentment towards me. Despite these concerns, I knew I had to accept it and move on. However, I also realized that this unexpected spotlight could potentially create challenges for me relating to the rest of the crew. As I prepared to board the Starship, I braced myself for any difficulties that may arise due to this situation.

I approached the captain and requested permission for the ship to leave the space station so we could test the laser control system. However, before proceeding, I suggested that two technicians, whom I had personally recommended, inspect the system for potential issues. The captain agreed, and we conducted a thorough examination of all controls. To my surprise, the technicians discovered evidence of deliberate sabotage and damage to crucial controls, rendering the system inoperable. We embarked on our journey the following day, so I asked if it would be possible to repair the laser. The technicians assured me they had all the necessary parts and would start repairs immediately, which was a huge relief. In light of this situation, I emphasized the need for confidentiality and insisted that only the captain and I should know about the ongoing repair efforts. I informed the captain about the details of the sabotage on the laser controls, and we both agreed to keep this incident under wraps until we could identify the culprit and their motives. I also asked about any recent personnel changes on board, to which the captain mentioned a civilian technician responsible for maintenance tasks was still present. Realizing the vulnerability of our laser controls, I proposed installing surveillance cameras to monitor any unauthorized access attempts. This would make it easier for us to catch any potential perpetrators who might try to manipulate the controls. As my mind raced with suspicion and fear, I confided in the captain that the recent sabotage on our ship was not a mere coincidence but rather a deliberate act perpetrated by an unknown enemy. I foresaw the possibility of an enemy ship waiting to attack us. To confirm my theory, I proposed that we be prepared for attack at the first transfer point of the wormhole, as it could provide an opportunity to catch any potential threats lying in ambush. With a sense of urgency and determination, I assured the captain that I had already alerted the Empress to our predicament, and she had graciously agreed to delay her departure by one day so we could take necessary security measures. The weight of responsibility and danger hung heavy in the air, but I knew we must act swiftly and decisively to protect ourselves and our mission.

As I shared my suspicions with the captain, a tense silence seemed to hang in the air. The possibility of deliberate sabotage weighed heavily on everyone's minds, signaling the potential presence of an enemy ship lurking nearby, waiting to attack us. To confirm this theory, I proposed that we journey through the first transfer point of the wormhole at total battle stations, as it could provide an opportunity to intercept any threats we may encounter. With determination in my voice, I assured the captain that I had already informed the Empress of our situation. Each passing moment was crucial as we prepared for what might be a dangerous expedition ahead. With the captain's adamant approval, we received orders to prepare the ship's crew for its imminent launch into the great unknown. The anticipation was palpable as we went through the necessary protocols and checks, knowing we would reach our initial wormhole transfer point in eight hours. I could feel my heart racing as I stood at the laser controls, ready and willing to face whatever challenges lay ahead.

As our ship navigated through the swirling vortex of the wormhole, I held on tight and braced myself for the sudden jolt and turbulence that always accompanied such a journey. My eyes were fixed on the viewport, watching in awe as stars became streaks of light and space warped around us.

But then, as quickly as it began, we emerged from the wormhole and were met with unexpected danger. An unknown enemy had appeared out of nowhere, firing two deadly missiles directly at our ship. Without hesitation, I aimed at the hostile Raider vessel and fired two laser shots with precision and skill. The first blast successfully neutralized both incoming missiles, ensuring the safety of our crew and our precious vessel.

My second shot hit the Raider ship's star drive, triggering a series of devastating explosions that led to its ultimate demise. Despite our cheers of triumph, we were all aware of the high possibility of encountering more enemies on our expedition through the empire. Yet, I had complete confidence in my fellow crew members and knew that we were prepared to confront any challenges that may come our way.

The perpetrators of these attacks have significant financial means and powerful connections at their disposal. They can easily supply professional assassins and skilled riders. We must bring this matter to the attention of the investigation department, promoting transparency and accountability in our actions. With their vast network and resources, it begs the question of what their next move will be.

After traveling through six different worlds, we finally arrived at the seventh. During their meeting, the Empress asked if I would be interested in attending an event following our visit. The planet is governed by a Baroness whom I had accompanied to a prestigious event where we prevented an attempt on the Empress's life by assassins. Grateful for the invitation, I accepted, feeling obligated due to the positive relationship I had developed with the Baroness during the event.

As I sat across from the Baroness, she proudly introduced me to her daughter again, who stood beside her. "I was hoping you two could develop a relationship," she said. Glancing at the daughter, I noticed how much she resembled her mother. She exuded grace and elegance, a product of her upbringing. "I appreciate the offer," I began, "but at this time, my duty to protect the Empress prevents me from forming any long-term relationships."

The Baroness nodded understandingly, disappointment evident but accepting of my answer. Being a figure of authority, she understood the demands of duty." I know," she replied, "Your commitment is admirable. Perhaps when circumstances allow, our paths may cross again."With gratitude, I offered a nod to acknowledge her understanding. For the remainder of the evening, we engaged in pleasant conversation. I bid farewell to the Baroness and her daughter as the event ended. On my journey home, my thoughts turned towards what the future held. The recent events - attempted sabotage of the laser control system and attack by an unknown enemy ship- were reminders of the constant danger faced by our empire. These thoughts left me with unease that lingered even after I reached home.

After returning to the Starship, I called for a meeting with the captain and our security team to discuss the recent events and their implications. We carefully studied the surveillance footage and analyzed data for any suspicious activity or anomalies that could have contributed to the sabotage. This was a well-planned and coordinated act of sabotage. It was likely carried out by individuals with inside knowledge of our ship's systems. We immediately implemented strict security protocols to prevent further breaches and unauthorized access. All civilian technicians underwent comprehensive background checks to ensure their loyalty and reliability. As we reinforced our defenses and heightened our vigilance, I felt a strong sense of urgency to uncover the truth behind the sabotage and bring those responsible to justice. The safety of not only the Empress but the entire empire was at stake, and it was our duty to protect it by thwarting any future threats and safeguarding the integrity of our starships.

Surrounded by my fellow officers and crew members on the bridge of the Starship, I braced myself for the challenges ahead. We were united in our mission to defend the empire and uphold its values of justice, honor, and duty. A sense of purpose and determination filled me. The adventure had just begun, and I was eager to see where destiny would lead us. However, despite my resolve, there was a lingering unease within me. Recent events had cast doubt over our mission, and I knew we needed to remain vigilant. On the bridge, I worked closely with the captain and security team to fortify our defenses and anticipate potential threats during our journey through the vast expanse of space. Every system was scrutinized to ensure that no vulnerabilities were left unchecked. Our ultimate goal was clear: to prevent any further attempts at sabotage and to protect the lives of everyone aboard the starship. As we delved deeper into our investigation, I couldn't help but feel a sense of urgency gnawing at me. Time was of the essence, and every moment wasted could mean the difference between success and failure. We combed through surveillance footage, analyzed data logs, and interrogated crew members in search of any clues that could lead us to the perpetrators. Amidst the chaos and uncertainty, one thing remained constant: my unwavering commitment to duty. The oath I had sworn to uphold weighed heavily on my shoulders, driving me forward even in the face of adversity. I knew that the safety of the Empress and the Empire depended on our ability to uncover the truth and neutralize the threat.

As the Starship hurtled through space, days turned into weeks, and tensions mounted among the weary crew. Every creak and groan of the ship's hull seemed to reverberate with a foreboding sense of danger lurking just beyond the stars. Yet, amidst the turmoil and fear, a bond began to form between the crew members - a sense of unity in the face of adversity. And then, finally, after what felt like an eternity, our perseverance paid off. A crucial piece of evidence surfaced, pointing us toward a suspect with ties to a notorious organization known for its nefarious activities. With this newfound lead, we wasted no time giving the information to the Empire investigation unit so they could launch a covert operation to apprehend the perpetrator. The air buzzed with anticipation as we prepared for what could be a decisive moment in our journey through the unknown depths of space.

Chapter 7

I decided to visit Admiral Astra, my trusted friend and confidante among the higher ranks of the fleet. Our bond had only grown stronger with each mission and victory we shared. Out of all the people I've ever worked with, her advice was always the most valuable to me."Admiral," I greeted with a respectful nod as I entered her office, "It's good to see you." She returned my greeting warmly and gestured for me to take a seat. "I'm glad. What's on your mind?" As I settled into the chair across from her desk, I couldn't help but let my serious expression show. "I just wanted to check in and see how you're doing." But before I could finish, Admiral Astra raised a hand, her expression now grave. "Commander, there's something important I need to tell you." I immediately sensed a shift in the atmosphere. "What is it?" I asked anxiously. Taking a deep breath, the Admiral met my gaze steadily. "I've decided to retire," she announced, her words heavy in the air. The news hit me like a punch to the stomach. Retirement? So soon? I couldn't even fathom the fleet without Admiral Astra leading them, guiding us through our most complex challenges. "But why?"

I managed to ask, disbelief coloring my voice. " I nodded slowly in understanding, though my mind was racing with mixed emotions. The weight of duty rested heavily on the Admiral's shoulders, her chest tight with pride and sorrow. With a heavy heart, she accepted that she had fulfilled her duty, though it was not without struggle and sacrifice. A bittersweet relief washed over her as she reflected on her accomplishments. Slowly, I nodded in understanding, though my mind was racing with emotions. Retirement meant more than just the end of an illustrious career—it also meant losing my closest ally and source of guidance and support. "I understand," I finally said, though my words felt hollow on my tongue. The Admiral reached across her desk and touched my arm reassuringly. "Pope, you have proven yourself time and time again. And don't forget, I will only be a subspace message away if you ever need advice." Despite her words, I couldn't shake the overwhelming feeling of loss. Of course, the fleet would continue without Admiral Astra, but it would never be quite the same for me.

"Admiral, have you thought about your retirement plans?" "I've been considering starting a medium-sized shipping company that would operate across galaxies. I aim to bring retired fleet officers and crew aboard, assuming I can secure the necessary funding." "It seems like you've thoroughly thought this through." "I've meticulously planned out all the details, but I'm still looking for a partner to help with the financial aspect." The idea presented had a lot of potential and promise for success. I'm interested in exploring the possibility of collaborating with you on this venture. I have significant savings in my account and am willing to invest in this project to help it grow and succeed. "Are you sure you're ready to be partners with me?" "I'm fully committed to moving forward with this collaboration as long as you're comfortable with me taking on a part-time role in the partnership." "I have no objections to your proposal. Let's take some time to discuss and finalize our plans over the next few months so we can both be on the same page and working towards a common goal." "That sounds like a great plan, and I'm excited about the opportunity to work together on this project. Our partnership has enormous potential and can bring our shared vision to life." As they parted ways, Pope couldn't help but think about what the future held for him, their project, and his enduring bond with his dear friend and mentor. The possibilities were endless, and he was eager to see how their collaboration would unfold in the coming days.

The following day, Pope took a stroll around the bustling city. The weight of his responsibilities temporarily lifted as he breathed in the crisp evening air and took in the sights and sounds of the lively streets. As I rounded the bend, his stroll was abruptly interrupted by a chaotic chorus of yells and cries up ahead. Intrigued, he hastened his pace and soon came upon a distressing scene. Two young women, their faces twisted with malice, had trapped a more petite figure against a wall. The victim cowered in fear as the bullies hurled insults and threats at her. Pope's commanding presence caused the two women to falter momentarily. "Enough," he stated firmly, his voice resonating with authority. The aggressors turned their attention to him, their expressions shifting from arrogance to defiance. "And who might you be?" one of them taunted. Pope's gaze hardened as he calmly told them he did not tolerate bullying. "Leave her alone." The bullies exchanged a sneering glance before bursting into mocking laughter. "Or what?" the other one jeered. "You gonna run crying to Mommy?" Pope remained composed and determined to stand up for the victims despite their cruel words.

"I warned you," he said quietly, his voice sharp and persistent. He raised his arm with a swift, practiced motion, and a sleek laser weapon materialized in his hand. The bullies' cruel laughter faltered as they watched, their eyes widening with disbelief at the unexpected turn of events. They took a cautious step back, uncertain how to react to this sudden display of power. Before they could gather their thoughts, Pope aimed the device at the ground and squeezed the trigger. A blinding light beam shot forth, melting a smoking hole into the solid concrete pavement. The acrid scent of burnt stone filled the air, causing the bullies to flinch and take another step back, their bravado quickly crumbling in the face of such a powerful demonstration."I am going to count to three," Pope's voice rang out, low but commanding. "If you are not gone by the time I reach three, that hole will be in one of you." The bullies' faces paled as they realized the gravity of the situation. Without another word, they turned on their heels and fled, disappearing into the shadows. Pope stood tall and unwavering, watching them go before turning his attention to the girl they had been tormenting. With a sense of relief, she looked up at him, her savior. "Are you alright?" he asked gently, offering her a reassuring smile. She nodded gratefully, "Thank you." "Absolutely," the Pope affirmed with empathy. His resolute declaration emphasized the importance of respecting everyone, as his compassionate and confident voice. His words echoed a stubborn belief in every individual's inherent value and dignity. "Remember, if you ever need help, don't hesitate to ask," Pope asked if he could accompany her to her desired location. She responded, mentioning that her workplace was the nearby real estate office. Intrigued, I asked if she was a real estate agent. However, she clarified that she was merely a secretary at the office.

We proceeded to the office, where I had the opportunity to meet her boss - a successful and charming real estate agent. As a skilled salesperson, she asked if I was interested in purchasing a new home or residence. I replied that while I might consider it in the future, it wasn't my current priority. In response, she kindly handed me her business card and encouraged me to contact her anytime to explore some properties.

Grateful for her offer, I thanked her and departed. It occurred to me that depending on how long I would remain in the fleet, I might need a place to call home. After taking in the sights and sounds of the city and getting acquainted with my surroundings, I made my way back to the castle.

As I stood guard at my post, a summons from the captain of the guard reached me. I made my way towards him, fully prepared to fulfill my duty and contribute to the safety of the Empire. The air was thick with curiosity and obligation as the captain began to relay a message that gave me a sense of purpose. Admiral Orian had handpicked me for an important assignment - to serve as Laser Fire control officer on one of their vessels. This opportunity was significant, for it emerged as an urgent response to a critical situation. The fleet required my expertise to ensure the secure transportation of a group of troopers needed to help suppress a growing rebellion on the volatile surface of planet Cotan. I accepted this vital mission, ready to do whatever it takes to protect and serve the Empire.

With my curiosity piqued by the unusual request, I couldn't resist inquiring about its origins. Much to my surprise, the captain revealed that it was Admiral Orian herself who had explicitly chosen me for this mission. My immediate reaction was skepticism and unease, given the tense history between the Admiral and myself. The thought crossed my mind that this assignment may hold ulterior motives, potentially even functioning as a trap. However, as a soldier bound by duty, I knew I had no choice but to follow orders and embark on this journey. Despite the nagging apprehension gnawing at me, I steeled myself to face whatever challenges lay ahead, determined to fulfill my duties with caution.

A surprise shot through my body as I stepped onto the ship's deck. My feet stopped mid-step, frozen by the imposing figure before me - Captain Lyra's commanding presence looming over me like a dark cloud. Memories of our previous journey flooded my mind, reminding me of our constant tension and animosity. It seemed nothing had changed.

With a sharp tone, she told the bridge crew I was not to leave the ship's safety and join the troopers in their upcoming battle on the distant planet. But deep down, I knew better than to trust her words. I could see right through her facade, recognizing the trap she had set for me. My instincts screamed at me, but I confidently stood my ground.

I ensured every crew member heard me when I said, "Not to worry, I know it's a trap." My bold defiance took aback the captain and her loyalists. They did not understand that my true calling was to fight alongside the troopers, to protect and defend them.

Confronted with a tough decision, I am standing at the intersection of following orders from our captain or following my own heart. It's a dilemma between mindlessly obeying authority and staying true to my beliefs and purpose. As I carefully consider my options, a sense of determination surges. Regardless of my chosen path, I will do so with unwavering courage and conviction. The choice to join the troopers in their battle could have tremendous consequences for me, potentially changing the course of my life. As I weigh the potential impact on this journey, I can't help but feel that it could be time for a change. As our ship descended into orbit around the planet, I eagerly joined the troopers in their designated area. They prepared to depart for the planet's surface, checking weapons and reviewing last-minute strategies. Excited and nervous, I approached the commanding officer in charge of this mission and explained my situation. She listened attentively before assuring me this would not be a long battle, as the opposing force was relatively small. Despite her suggestion to remain on the ship, I couldn't shake off my determination to join her and the troopers on the planet below—the thrill of adventure and desire to contribute overwhelmed any doubts or fears I may have had. Despite the prestige and privileges that came with being an officer, my heart has always belonged to the life of a combat infantry soldier. It is a calling that I have embraced and intend to carry out until my last breath. As we made our way towards the shuttle, adrenaline surged through my veins in anticipation of the upcoming mission - to quell the uprising on the planet's surface. The journey down was tense, but as we descended, it became clear that the rebels had underestimated our group's size and strength. They stood no chance against our well-trained and well-equipped forces. In a display of surrender, they waved a white flag, defeated. The operation concluded swiftly and efficiently, leaving us with a sense of suspicion. It soon became apparent that our captain had orchestrated this scenario to test my loyalty and obedience to direct orders. My fate within the Empire now hangs in the balance - will I be rewarded or punished for my actions? Only time will tell.

As I stepped back onto the ship, my heart was pounding. I knew I was in trouble for disobeying a direct order, and sure enough, I was immediately arrested and confined to my quarters until we returned to fleet headquarters. The weight of what I had done sat heavily on my shoulders as I waited anxiously for when I would have to face Admiral Orion.

I knew what was coming when we docked at the space station. My footsteps echoed through the metallic corridors as I went to the Admiral's office. As soon as I entered, she fixed me sternly and said, "This is the second time you have disobeyed a direct order, Pope. You are facing a court-martial." The words hit me like a weight, dragging my heart even further. But then something unexpected happened. Instead of cowering under her authoritative gaze, I straightened my stance and spoke confidently. "I don't think so, Admiral," I said firmly. "I believe I will opt for retirement instead." To my surprise, she didn't immediately shut down this suggestion. Instead, she countered, "That's not an option, Pope." The tension in the room crackled like electricity as we both stood our ground, determined not to back down. But I had a trump card up my sleeve. "Admiral, I'd like you to listen to something," I said as I played her a recording of my reply when the captain had ordered me not to go to the planet with the troopers. Her expression changed from one of dominance to one of realization as she listened."How do you think this will go over at my court-martial?" I asked pointedly. She knew that I had her cornered, and to save face, she would have to go along with my decision to retire. After some negotiation, we agreed that a Section 6 retirement-type release from the fleet would be best for both parties. This type of retirement ensured that I would never be reinstated in the fleet unless I returned with written, signed papers by a fleet Admiral for a time not exceeding six months or less.

Relieved and grateful, I watched the Admiral draw up the necessary documents. We both signed them and then I departed, ready to start a new chapter of my life outside of the fleet.

Upon my return to the castle, I immediately contacted Admiral Astra and explained my predicament. "John, did you anticipate this situation?" she inquired. "I did and found a way to avoid a court-martial," I replied confidently. "That's good news. It looks like we now have a full-time partner for our endeavors," she said with satisfaction. "For now, I will need to find a place to live - perhaps a hotel," I stated. To my surprise, she offered me an apartment she had available until I could secure a more permanent residence. "Thank you," I expressed my gratitude. "I'll send you the address and entry code," she informed me before ending the call. When I arrived at the castle, the captain of the guard was surprised by my sudden retirement. His demeanor softened as she warmly greeted me and praised my years of service. I handed her the necessary paperwork. "Commander, I will inform the Empress of your departure, but I must warn you, she won't be pleased," he cautioned. "I understand. I'll gather my belongings and make arrangements to leave," I said, preparing for the uncertain future.

As I was leaving, Admiral Astra called me and asked about the progress of my Starship. During our last exchange, I informed her they had finished installing the laser fire control system and the double missile firing units. She then shared some information about a bounty policy specifically targeting Rotons and suggested I look into it due to my vendetta against them for their actions on Earth. Furthermore, she mentioned the availability of two small freighters in storage from a now-defunct company, which could be purchased at a favorable price to help us start our business. She thought Altaira, the Starship manufacturer, might be able to assist in getting these ships back in working condition. I promised to speak with Altaira and update her on any developments. After the call with Admiral Astra, I considered the possibilities and challenges of seeking revenge against the Rotons while securing more resources for our mission. I called Altaira to update her on my situation with the fleet and inquire about my ship's status. She invited me to her apartment above the facility for further discussion tonight at 7:30 pm.

On my way to meet with Altaira, I quickly stopped by my apartment to change into something casual. The condo had a cozy bedroom, spacious living room, and well-equipped compact kitchen. After stowing my belongings, I made my way to Altaira's place. She greeted me warmly with a hug and a kiss, expressing her delight in seeing me. As we sat at the table, we delved into the interior plans for my new Starship. The designs were exceptional, and I had no doubts about approving them. I confided in her about my current struggles within the fleet and my decision to retire. She listened attentively, offering words of understanding and support. She mentioned that perhaps this change was for the best, given the circumstances. I then shared with her the exciting news of my collaboration with the Admiral to establish a small-scale intergalactic shipping company. We were finalizing the acquisition of two medium-sized freighters sitting in storage for a few years after their previous company went out of business. We expressed our desire for her maintenance division to bring these ships up to top-notch condition and ensure they were fully functional. She readily agreed, mentioning that her team could assist as they were not operating fully. It was comforting to know that we had her support in this venture.

The idea of introducing a new AI system onto my ship was raised, and suddenly, the atmosphere grew heavy with significance. My limited experience in controlling Starships was brought up as a critical issue, emphasizing the seriousness of the situation. The Empire's staunch policy against granting full autonomy to AI systems only underscored the severity of the problem. The potential risks and dangers posed by such autonomy were clear – the emergence of independent entities capable of taking control of powerful Starships. The notion of equipping my ship with an AI system that defied these limitations was not only a direct violation of Empire policy and regulations but also carried severe repercussions if discovered. Despite the potential dangers, Altaira posed a plan to reduce possible risks. She will equip my new Starship with cutting-edge AI technology and two backup systems as a precaution. This strategy would allow me to switch to the standard backups in case of an Empire inspection, concealing the true capabilities of the advanced AI and avoiding potential consequences. As I grappled with the implications and stakes, my fiend questioned my determination, seeking assurance of my commitment to proceed with this plan. Her words hung heavy in the air, prompting a moment of deep introspection as I considered all possible outcomes and consequences of our actions.

Leaning forward, I met her gaze with unwavering determination. "I need you to understand," I began, my words carefully measured yet filled with earnestness, "that going through with our agreement is not a decision I make lightly. It's the only way to reach my home planet and find my path back home."Her expression was a mix of understanding and concern as she nodded in response."However," I continued, my voice firm, "I am fully aware of the gravity of this situation. And I am prepared to take full responsibility for any consequences arising from our arrangement."A heavy moment of silence engulfed us, the weight of our words palpable in the air."I won't involve you in this," I declared, my tone resolute. "You have no part in it. I'll bear the burden alone and ensure your complete non-involvement."

Thank you," she whispered, her voice barely audible. As if breaking the tense atmosphere, she shifted slightly in her seat. "Your ship will be ready for evaluation in approximately three weeks," she told me, her professional demeanor returning."Perfect," I replied, a genuine sense of relief washing over me. "Thank you for everything."With the weighty discussion behind us, a lightness settled over the room. We exchanged a small smile, silently agreeing to momentarily set aside the seriousness of our dealings. The remainder of the evening unfolded more relaxed as we indulged in lighthearted activities, finding solace in each other's company amidst the uncertainty of our shared journey.

Chapter 8

The next day, Pope and Admiral Astra convened for their planning session, both brimming with anticipation for the task ahead. "Alright, let's dive in," Commander Pope initiated, his voice resonating with purpose. "We need a comprehensive strategy that addresses every facet of this venture, from logistics to security. "Agreed," Admiral Astra affirmed firmly, her gaze fixed on the star map sprawled before them. "Our priority should be establishing secure trade routes. We can't afford any breaches or piracy."Commander Pope gestured towards the intricate network of stars and routes depicted on the map. "Security measures are paramount, but we must also prioritize efficiency. What's our plan for streamlining the shipping process?"

"We'll need cutting-edge cargo vessels outfitted with the latest navigation and propulsion systems," Commander Pope replied decisively. "Additionally, implementing a centralized tracking system to monitor shipments in real-time will be indispensable."Admiral Astra nodded in agreement, her mind already racing with ideas. "Absolutely. In addition, forging strategic partnerships with larger shipping entities will bolster our operations and expand our reach."

As the hours passed, the two leaders delved deeper into the intricacies of their plan, their synergy palpable as they seamlessly bounced ideas off each other. It became evident that Commander Pope and Admiral Astra formed a formidable team, their commitment to the success of an Intergalactic Shipping Co. unwavering. As the meeting drew close, a sense of satisfaction lingered. Pope and Admiral Lee exchanged a knowing nod, silently acknowledging the challenges ahead. Yet, they were undeterred, fueled by their shared vision and determination to see their endeavor through with meticulous planning and unwavering resolve.

"By the way, Pope, there's more," Admiral Astra interjected, her tone conveying intrigue. "I've taken the initiative to delve into the matter of the two mid-sized ships that have been in storage for quite some time now. I've arranged a meeting with the bank, which has come into possession of these vessels following the collapse of the previous company." she paused briefly, allowing the significance of her words to sink in before continuing. "Once I obtain a purchase price for the ships, I'll promptly inform you. From there, we can scrutinize this potential acquisition's financial implications and requirements. It could be a valuable addition to our fleet, but we must carefully assess all angles before proceeding."

After the Admiral departed, I pondered my next move. Removing my fleet uniform, I rummaged through the pockets and stumbled upon a real estate card from a peculiar encounter during a stroll through the city. Recognizing its potential significance, I resolved to explore the options it presented. After a refreshing shower, I set out towards the real estate office. I contemplated the prospect of securing my own home.

I felt a pressing need to find a residence that could shield me from potential threats posed by the Assassin's Guild's retribution. Upon arriving at the real estate office, I explained to the agent my requirement for a home offering high security and seclusion. She promptly began presenting various options tailored to my specific needs. After inspecting several properties, one in particular captured my interest - an isolated residence nestled approximately 30 miles along the ocean coast.

The agent informed me that an individual with unique tastes and a strong emphasis on privacy and security constructed this property.

It features four bedrooms, an ample living space, an indoor pool, and various thoughtful amenities to provide a sanctuary of comfort and tranquility. Additionally, it includes a hangar suitable for storing a small shuttlecraft. What set this home apart was its advanced security system, with cameras, motion sensors surrounding the property, and a comprehensive monitoring station inside the house.

Despite its allure, one drawback was its exposure to frequent strong winds and lightning storms. The property was meticulously planned and equipped with advanced technology to withstand extreme weather conditions. Intrigued by the prospect of residing in such a resilient and well-prepared sanctuary, I expressed my desire to view the property immediately. The agent explained that she needed the owner's security code but assured me they could arrange a shuttlecraft to transport us, as no roads were leading to the property. I agreed, saying, "Yes, please inform me when we can visit it." Yet, as I exited the office, a nagging doubt lingered in my mind. Was this indeed the right decision? Only time will tell.

Two days had elapsed since John's conversation with Rowe, the real estate agent. so when his Comm. finally rang, he eagerly snatched it up. "John, I've got some good news," the agent's voice came through the receiver. "I've arranged for us to fly out to the residence you've been eyeing. Are you ready?"John confirmed his readiness with a quick affirmative. Before long, they were soaring toward the isolated abode, anticipation in the air. As the shuttlecraft descended, the residence emerged into view, perched gracefully on the shoreline.

Stepping onto the grounds, John followed the agent as they made their way inside, the grandeur of the property unfolding before them. The interior exceeded even his wildest expectations. Four expansive bedrooms, each tastefully furnished, welcomed them with open arms. The pièce de résistance, however, was the indoor swimming pool, boasting large observation windows that offered sweeping vistas of the boundless sea and the endless horizon beyond.

As they completed their inspection and began their journey back, the agent smiled at John. "So, what do you think?""It's perfect,". "But the price..." agent nodded knowingly. "I understand, John. The asking price is 120,000." "I'm just not willing to pay that much," he admitted. "But I'm prepared to offer 80,000." The agent's expression softened. "I'll be honest, John. That might be a hard sell, but I'll present it to the client. Thank you for considering it." Uncertainty filled John's mind as they went their separate paths, leaving him with a sense of uneasiness about the acceptance of his offer. Only the passage of time would reveal the outcome. Upon my return to the real estate office, after a week of eager anticipation, exciting news awaited me: The client agreed to my proposal of 80,000. Expressing my satisfaction, I wasted no time in requesting the necessary paperwork. With eagerness coursing through my veins, I eagerly awaited the opportunity to sign it and transfer the funds to the agency's account. While the timeline for completing the transaction might be longer than expected, viewing it positively, this extended timeframe allows for thorough attention to detail. I inquired about hiring a housekeeper and cook to ensure the smooth operation of my new home. The agent regretfully informed me that such services fell beyond her scope of expertise and suggested seeking suitable candidates online. Grateful for her guidance, I bid farewell and exited the bustling street.

As I navigated the sidewalk, a familiar face caught my eye – the young girl I had previously rescued from a group of bullies. Approaching me with a sparkle in her eye, she eagerly relayed that she and her partner were keen to take on the responsibilities of housekeeping and cooking at my new residence. Intrigued by their proposal, I questioned whether they were comfortable with the isolated location. To my surprise, she assured me that it was an ideal fit for them, tired as they were of facing discrimination due to their personal preferences. Recognizing their enthusiasm and potential, I expressed genuine interest in their services and requested their contact information. Promising to reach out as soon as all necessary arrangements were in place, I proposed a discussion to outline the details of their role as my housekeeper and cook. Grateful for their eagerness and the opportunity to support them, I thanked them sincerely and look forward to our future.

A week later, Altaira informed me that my Starship was ready for a test launch. Standing before it, I couldn't help but feel a sense of excitement and anticipation. This Starship was not just any ordinary vessel; it was my spacecraft. With a confident smile, she asked if we were ready for the shakedown run. I replied eagerly, expressing my enthusiasm for the upcoming tests. She assured me that the AI system had undergone extensive testing and that the laser fire control system exceeded expectations. The simulated targeting software was also fully prepared for action. The Starship, named the Little Star, was special to me as it represented my opportunity to return home. Determined, I urged everyone not to keep the Starship waiting and proceeded towards the control section with a clear purpose. Once on board, I settled into the captain's chair, feeling the vibrations of the ship's engines beneath me. I commanded the AI to initiate the shakedown sequence, ready to embark on this journey. The AI, a sophisticated neural network, sprang to life, her virtual presence on the viewscreen before me. "Shakedown sequence initiated, Captain," she replied in her smooth, synthesized voice. With a gentle button push, the Little Star glided gracefully out of the docking bay and into the vast expanse of space. Stars streaked by in a blur as we accelerated to cruising speed, the ship responding effortlessly to my commands."Engage laser fire

Before our departure, Altaira disclosed an additional unique feature of my ship. Its upgraded star drive would enable the vessel to travel 1.5 to 1.7 times faster than any other Starship in the Empire presently. She emphasized the importance of keeping this information confidential, as she did not want anyone else to be aware of the upgrade. She would receive data from my Starship to ensure everything was functioning as intended. As a gesture of goodwill, she waived the final payment for the ship, allowing me to have this advanced star drive. It was clear to me that the secrecy surrounding this upgrade was crucial, as there would be many individuals eager to obtain the new design of the star drive. I assured her I understood the significance of keeping this information private, acknowledging all the assistance she had provided me.

Following the successful trial of my vessel, Admiral Astra happily notified me that the purchase of the two medium-sized Starship freighters had been marking a significant milestone in our ventures. I felt a surge of excitement. The prospect of expanding our fleet, especially with the ships docked right next to my personal Starship at bay 14 and 15. The Admiral's next piece of news immediately captured my attention. He relayed a request from a passenger ship needing an escort through a dangerous wormhole transfer point to planet Solris. The dangers posed by previous Raider attacks made the journey treacherous, and the Empire's fleet was unavailable due to their commitments to border control."Why don't they request an escort from the Empire's fleet?" I inquired, puzzled by the situation. The Admiral explained the fleet's current engagements and the unavailability of resources to spare for escort duties. However, he mentioned that the passenger ship was willing to pay a premium for our services, mainly because of my ship's advanced laser control firing system. The opportunity to bolster our reputation as a new freighting company in the Empire was enticing."Alright, let's proceed," I decided without hesitation. "Inform them that I'll be their escort." Good, thanks, John. I'll convey the message to them and update you on when this mission will occur," the Admiral assured me. With the decision made, I began preparations for the escort mission, eager to showcase our capabilities and solidify our standing in the Empire's freighter community.

I briefed my AI Ally on the upcoming escort mission, which involved meeting the passenger ship at the entrance of Wormhole 21. Our task is to guide them safely through the wormhole. I emphasized the importance of not getting too far ahead, expressing my concern about potential raiders lurking in wait. I will position myself at the laser control pod before we exit to take action as we near the exit point. Approaching the wormhole, I relayed instructions to the captain of the passenger ship, advising them to follow closely behind us. With hopes for a smooth and uneventful journey, I prepared for any potential threats that may arise during our passage through the wormhole transfer section.

As we exited the wormhole, a raider ship lying in wait immediately targeted us at the wormhole transfer point. Swiftly responding, we took action. I managed to intercept the missile launched towards us, preventing any harm to our vessel. Determined to retaliate, I aimed my laser at the stardrive section of the Raider's stardrive system, hoping to deactivate it. Although the damage inflicted was minimal, it was enough to cause the raider ship to falter and retreat. With the raider ship retreating, the passenger ship emerged from the wormhole and relayed a message: they must go on, and I would pursue the Raider and eliminate it once and for all. I ordered Ally that we should track down the Raider and put an end to its threat. We swiftly followed its path, closing in on it as it sought refuge near a massive asteroid. Seizing the opportunity, I aimed my laser again, targeting the raider ship stardrive. The laser struck its mark, causing a chain reaction that resulted in the raider ship exploding into countless fragments, scattering across space. The destruction of the stardrives of the raider ship unleashed a display of light and energy. The composition of the stardrives remained a mystery to me, but their demise was undeniably impressive.

Allie informed me that her sensors had picked up on some structure on the asteroid, leading us to believe it was the Raider Homebase. As we neared the asteroid, I inquired about the possibility of landing so I could investigate further. Allie confirmed that we could land, but I would need to don my space suit before disembarking due to the lack of a breathable atmosphere. Once suited up, I explored the installation, reaching a set of sealed doors. I asked Allie if she could hack into the site's computer system to gain access, and she successfully opened the airlock for me. Stepping inside, I was relieved to find a breathable environment, which allowed me to remove my helmet. The facility intended to cater to a specific group of people. No personnel were here; they must have been on the Raider ship. I came across crates of missiles, all lacking the required serial numbers. The unauthorized rockets were obtained illegally rather than being sanctioned by the Empire. After completing my investigation, I returned to the ship and decided not to report my findings to the Empire. Instead, I opted to keep the location of the raider outpost a secret for potential future use. I noted the coordinates, ensuring we could revisit the site if necessary before departing through the wormhole to rendezvous with the passenger ship.

Upon our safe return to Space Station 50, I entered our newly assigned office, filled with personnel anxiously awaiting their interviews with the Admiral. Eager to share the good news, I quickly informed the Admiral about the successful delivery of all passengers to their intended destination. She expressed her satisfaction, acknowledging the positive impact this would have on our reputation. However, I couldn't help but mention that I had encountered a Raider at the transfer point and had taken it down. The incident validated the passenger company's concern about the potential risk at that particular transfer point. The Admiral, impressed by my actions, expressed her gratitude. I offered to transfer the bonus for taking down the Raider to the company account. Surprised by my generosity, Pope insisted, stating that he wanted the company to benefit. Grateful for my support, She thanked me for my kind gesture. Before concluding our conversation, the Admiral informed me about an upcoming meeting with the owners of three major shipping companies. The purpose of the meeting was to discuss potential collaborations that could benefit all parties involved.

The following week, a meeting with the owners of the three major shipping companies occurred. As they delved into discussions about potential collaborations."We've been considering a mutual relationship," John began, his voice steady and persuasive. "Our fleet consists of smaller ships, perfect for handling shipments that might not be economically viable for your larger vessels. We propose taking on these smaller shipments, sharing the shipping costs at 70 to 30 percent."The owners exchanged glances, considering the proposition. One of them leaned forward, her expression thoughtful. "And in return, if you happen to receive an order that exceeds the capacity of your medium-sized ships, you'd transfer it to us?"John nodded. "Exactly. We recognize our limitations and aim to complement each other's strengths. A discussion ensued, punctuated by questions, calculations, and scenarios. Yet, amidst the negotiations, there was an air of mutual respect and understanding. John emphasized their commitment to hiring retired fleet personnel, assuring the owners that they wouldn't hire their employees. All parties came to a mutual understanding and reached a consensus. Smiles illuminated the faces of all those present as they greeted each other with handshakes. It was a win-win situation, promising a prosperous future in the shipping industry for all involved. As the meeting concluded, each party departed satisfied.

Now that Pope has finally closed on his new house and settled in, I've also brought two remarkable women eager to work as housekeepers and cooks on board. We're currently busy cleaning every nook and cranny of the house and ensuring the security system is operational, which runs along the entire perimeter of the property is in perfect working order. The ladies do a fantastic job and seem content as they do their daily tasks. It's hard to believe we've lived here for about five weeks!

Over time, while collaborating with the Admiral in managing the shipping company and settling into my new residence, a sense of normalcy began to set in. The two women I had employed as cooks and housekeepers gradually grew closer to me, akin to sisters, forming a solid bond. To combat feelings of isolation and monotony in the secluded locale, I became a premium theater member, securing a private box for all their performances. Attending the theater became a means of coping with the seclusion, providing a monthly outing for the three of us to enjoy a show or musical together. Initially, we faced some unwelcome remarks from others in the theater community. However, I swiftly put an end to these comments by asserting my identity and reputation, prompting a shift in behavior towards us. The ambiance became more pleasant, and I received respectful treatment from everyone in attendance. After spending a considerable amount of time together, I consulted a lawyer to explore the possibility of legally adopting the two women as my sisters and ensuring that they would inherit my estate in case of my demise. This decision seemed prudent given the risks associated with my Laser Fire control officer and combat soldier role. The legal proceedings concluded, resulting in the official adoption of the two women who are now my sisters. Welcoming a new family to support me further solidified my feeling of connection and security within the neighborhood. They provided me with a support system in the face of the challenges I encountered in my work.

John, there is a call for you from Admiral Vega." Thanks, Admiral. Congratulations on your recent promotion to Admiral of the fleet. " Thank you. The Empress has requested your presence on Tyron to attend a meeting with the Admiak. The Empress believes your attendance at the meeting is crucial. However, the main reason for your attendance is that the Subterranean society is predominantly male-dominated. By accompanying the Empress, your presence would greatly aid the negotiations and ensure a smoother interaction between the two parties in response to your request for paperwork regarding retirement policies. I will complete the required documentation." "Without the proper paperwork I must have, there is a possibility of being reenlisted in the fleet full-time, which I believe is not my intention." "Considering the circumstances, I understand you may feel reluctant to return to uniform temporarily." "Admiral, however, it would be greatly appreciated if you could send the paperwork with your signature per the retirement policy. I am committed to helping the empire whenever I am needed. I appreciate your understanding. Just let me know when to report." "Will du john have a good day. "

Commander Poke and Empress Lasre found themselves in a crucial negotiation with the Admiak, focusing on the trade of Rexon, a rare mineral vital for star drive construction. The Admiak, aware of the mineral's significance, initially hesitated to part with their abundant supply, leading to intricate discussions and careful considerations. Following the successful negotiation with the Admiak, attention shifted towards establishing a meeting with the Rotons to address border security concerns. Given the proximity of Rotons' territories to the Admiak Empire, ensuring peaceful relations was paramount for regional stability, presenting a challenging yet essential task for the Admiak Empire delegates. Despite the potential challenges in negotiating with the Rotons, the Empire's Subterranean agents told Commander Poke and Empress Lasre to try securing a meeting to discuss mutual concerns and possible cooperation in border defense. The Galuten Empire's commitment to peace through cooperation and diplomacy highlighted its dedication to a stable and prosperous future for all involved in interstellar politics and trade. The Admiak agreed to try to set up the meeting as requested by the Empire. The Empire will receive information regarding the timing of the conference. If the Rotons agree, we will return.

Upon our departure, the chief negotiator discreetly beckoned me over. He disclosed that despite their lack of trust in the Rotons, they had established a partnership with them, with surveillance measures in place. He inquired about the Empress's potential interest in forming a pact of resistance, offering to augment the supply of Rexon ora to the Empire. When asked why he hadn't broached the subject during the official meeting, he admitted that their society was unaccustomed to negotiating with women, preferring to engage solely with men. Acknowledging this cultural barrier, I assured him I would relay the proposal to the Empress during our journey back to the Empire. As we returned, I updated the Empress about my unexpected meeting with the chief negotiator. I clarified the customs of their society. This revelation came as a surprise to her, and she promised to consider it. The Admiak said they had arranged a meeting with the Roton in two weeks.

We are now on our way to the meeting with the Roton. I was stationed at the Laser Fire Control of the Empire ship as we made our way towards the Subtrayene Federation Capital planet. The task was negotiating a peace treaty with the Rotons, a species notorious for their turbulent history with the Empire. As the vessel approached its destination, it encountered a treacherous asteroid field. Out of nowhere, two Roton ships emerged from the darkness between the asteroids, disrupting the peaceful space. Without hesitation, these hostile ships fired two rockets directly at the Empire vessel. Commander Pope, quick to respond to the imminent danger, focused intently on the incoming projectiles. With the ship's advanced Laser systems, a formidable burst of energy was released, successfully intercepting the rockets and preventing any harm to the ship. However, Commander Pope was not content with just defending the ship. The Roton ships were under constant attack, with laser blasts raining down on them without pause

. The space around them crackled with energy as the beams of light pierced through the emptiness, hitting their intended targets with exceptional accuracy. The Roton vessels, caught off guard by the Empire ship's fierce counterattack, were quickly overpowered by the relentless assault. In succession, the Roton ships succumbed to the overpowering firepower, their hulls punctured and consumed by flames. With the enemy defeated, the empire ship altered its course towards the Subtrayene Federation, continuing its journey toward peace negotiations. Pope told the Empress, "This was a planned ambush by the Rotons negotiating team. They will pay for this." Both the Empress and the Admiral were in shock over the past attack by the Rotons. No one knew what to expect at the negotiations.

The atmosphere in the negotiating chamber was tense as representatives from the Empire and the Rotons faced each other. The Admiak delegate, a stern and imposing figure in a sleek uniform, introduced the two Roton representatives, attempting to establish a sense of formality. However, before the formalities could fully settle in, Commander Pope, the outspoken officer from the Empire, shattered the uneasy silence. His voice filled with disdain as he accused the Rotons of orchestrating a treacherous ambush aimed at the Empress. The weight of his accusation hung in the air, creating a hatred that seemed to thicken with each passing moment. In a sudden and shocking turn of events, the two Roton representatives reacted aggressively, their hands reaching for concealed weapons. But Pope, ever vigilant, was already one step ahead. With lightning-fast reflexes, he swiftly drew his laser and fired, hitting both Rotons square in the head. The room erupted into chaos as the Rotons exploded, their heads splattering the chamber with dense green and yellow slime. The gruesome spectacle left everyone in stunned silence, their minds struggling to process the horrifying scene that had unfolded before them. Amidst the shocked silence, the Admiak Federation representative broke the stillness with his steady voice. Despite the chaos, he remained composed, his eyes betraying a hint of relief. "I'm glad you took decisive action," he admitted coolly, acknowledging Pope's swift response. His words carried a heavyweight in the air as a stark reminder of the delicate balance of power in the galaxy. With a collective nod, the delegates agreed to relocate to a new meeting room, leaving the cleanup to the designated team. As they negotiated, the goal of a mutual defiance treaty between the Admrik and the Empire remained at the forefront of their minds.

The Empress relayed to the Representative that the Empire was willing to enter a treaty with the Federation. Commander Pope was appointed to lead the negotiations for the treaty and the acquisition of resources upon his return. The unexpected events caught me off guard, but I had no option but to accept the task. While returning to their homeland, the Empress briefed Commander Pope on the forthcoming treaty and the necessary resources to be ready in two weeks. The treaty could be presented by him to their associated Federation, granting him the opportunity to do so. The Empress asked Commander Pope to tell her when he was ready to fulfill his duties, reassuring him of her unwavering support.

Upon receiving the message regarding the finalized treaty paperwork and the amount of Rexon ore needed for stardrives, Commander Pope immediately sprang into action. He promptly arranged a meeting with the three prominent owners of the major shipping companies to discuss the importance of the treaty. Together, they appointed a representative to accompany Commander Pope on his journey to the Federation, showing their commitment to the cause.

The following day, the small delegation embarked on their journey towards the Admiak Federation star system, encountering no significant hurdles. Their travel was smooth and uneventful, allowing them to arrive at their destination safely and in good spirits. Upon reaching the Federation, the leaders of the five planets warmly welcomed them, setting a positive tone for the upcoming discussions.

Commander Pope wasted no time presenting the treaty paperwork to the Federation leaders, who expressed their satisfaction and promptly signed the agreement. The event concluded with the mission's successful accomplishment, showcasing the efficient teamwork between the Empire and the Federation. Additionally, representatives from the shipping companies engaged in productive discussions with Federation authorities, laying the groundwork for potential future trade agreements that would benefit both parties.

As the discussions progressed, it became evident that both sides were eager to establish a mutually beneficial relationship. The initiation of a new era of cooperation between the Empire and the Federation began with the official implementation of the treaty and the establishment of open communication channels. Before his departure, Pope participated in a site meeting alongside Admiak Agens. During this meeting, Commander Pope shared the exciting news that the Empress had taken the initiative to upgrade two stored older Starships destroyers, intending to present them as a generous gift to the Federation as a symbol of goodwill. Overwhelmed with gratitude, Altairak expressed their heartfelt appreciation to the Empress. Commander Pope and his delegation returned home with

their accomplishments, recognizing their vital role in strengthening intergalactic relations and fostering positive interactions between the two entities.

Stepping off the Starship, Commander John Pope felt relief wash over him. Pope navigated the tense mission of brokering delicate treaty terms between the Federation and the Empire. However, he could finally exhale now that he held the signed treaty. As he entered the meeting with the Empress, Pope greeted her with a slight bow and presented the finalized agreement between their systems. The Empress graciously received the treaty, her eyes showing relief and gratitude as she smiled. She commended Commander Pope for his exemplary efforts on behalf of the Empire, acknowledging that the treaty represented a new chapter of cooperation and understanding in their shared history. With the treaty safely in the Empress's hands, Commander Pope expressed his gratitude to the Representative from Galactic Shipping Co., the company that had facilitated his journey. He thanked them for their service, recognizing their efficiency and professionalism as instrumental to the mission's success. With pleasantries exchanged and duties fulfilled, Commander John Pope went to his office at Star Shipping Co. He wanted to meet his partner Admiral Astra and discuss his trip to the Federation. Also, I want to see the two new star shipping ships.

Chapter 9

With excitement coursing through my veins, I set off on a stroll around the perimeter of my new property. The lush greenery and sparkling ocean vistas were a welcome change from the cramped confines of our spaceship. Walking along the sandy beach, I couldn't shake the feeling that someone or something was watching me. Brushing it off as mere nerves, I continued until I reached the end of the fence line. There, perched atop a massive boulder, I took in the breathtaking view of the ocean. Suddenly, a blur of movement caught my eye, and before I knew it, a creature unlike anything I had ever seen emerged from the dense tree line. It was like an earth panther but much more significant - at least five to seven times its size. We locked eyes, both curious and cautious about each other's presence. Despite the instinctual fear coursing through my body, I couldn't help but feel a strange connection to this magnificent being. As if sensing my thoughts, it turned away and gracefully retreated into the shelter of the trees. At that moment, I knew our encounter was just the beginning - our paths would cross again. I felt grateful for this extraordinary journey as I stood there lost in thought, marveling at this wondrous creature and all the surprises that awaited me in this new world. The possibilities seemed endless, and with each passing day, I could sense that my life would never be dull again.

I sat in my secluded home, surrounded by the latest high-tech security. The perimeter, with a fence lined with sensors and cameras, ensured that nothing could escape his property when he heard the alarm blaring. Pope sprang into action. He rushed to the security console, his mind racing through the possibilities of what could have triggered the intrusion alarm. He accessed the live feed from the perimeter cameras with a few keystrokes. His eyes scanned the monitors, looking for any movement or disturbance. There, in the corner of one screen, he spotted it- two shadowy figures moving stealthily along the edge of the fence.

Pope's trained ear picked up the faint sound of movement outside his secluded home. As he crept toward the front door, he activated the motion sensors that would reveal any intruders. Sure enough, two figures moved stealthily across his yard. Without hesitation, Pope retrieved his M35 rifle and positioned himself on the upper level of his home, where he had a clear view of his entire property. Through his scope, he saw the intruders approaching his property. His heart raced with adrenaline as he prepared to defend his sanctuary. The first figure fell with a single shot, but the second fired back. Pope quickly took him down before descending to check the identities of the bodies. His blood ran cold as he saw the assassin's tattoos on their skin—payback for stopping the Empress and the Highpristes' assassination attempts.

Pope clenched his jaw in frustration at the constant danger that surrounded him. But as he reflected on the events of the evening, he also felt a sense of pride. He had successfully defended his home once again, proving that he was willing to do whatever it took to protect what mattered most to him - his sanctuary amid chaos.

After examining the two corpses of the assassins, I quickly contacted the Empire's law enforcement. They arrived promptly in their shuttles. To my surprise, the inspector with them was the same person who had questioned me at the Empress's banquet, where I had taken down the other two attackers. She commented on my hostility towards the Assassin's Guild, and I replied that perhaps they should avoid crossing paths with me since they always seem to lose when we meet. I was intrigued by what became of the bodies, so I inquired about their fate. To my surprise, I learned that after the autopsy, they sent the bodies back to the Guild for burial. I asked for more information about this mysterious group's location. The inspector revealed that their headquarters were on the planet Ixadus, providing me with valuable information I could use to my advantage. With this knowledge, I made a mental note to contact them and give them a stern warning. I promised to make it clear that any future attempts on my life or threats against my family would have severe consequences. Fueled by determination, I prepared to confront the guild and ensure my safety and that of my loved ones.

CENTURIES AGO, THE enigmatic Guild was formed, shrouded in secrecy, and operates in the shadows with an air of mystery. Renowned for its precision and discretion, its members are feared and respected. The Guild operates under a strict hierarchical structure:

1. Grand Master: The authority overseeing all operations and strategic decisions from the shadows. Their identity is closely guarded, known only to a select few.

2. Assassins: These elite guild members undergo extensive combat, stealth, and infiltration training. Operating alone or in small teams, they execute missions with unparalleled precision and discretion.

3. Informants and Spies: Operating in the underbelly of society, these individuals excel at gathering intelligence, identifying targets, and providing crucial information to the assassins. Their skills in disguise and manipulation make them invaluable assets.

4. As the Guild is known, the Shadow's Edge accepts contracts from various sources, including affluent clients, political factions, and criminal syndicates. The assignments they undertake encompass a broad spectrum, ranging from the elimination of high-profile targets

to the acquisition of sensitive information and the disruption of rival operations.

FOR THE PAST TWO WEEKS, I had relentlessly searched for clues, scouring the depths of the Internet and calling in favors from allies across the Empire. Finally, my efforts paid off as I discovered the elusive communication channels to the Assassins' leader. I took a deep breath before dialing the number, mentally preparing myself for the encounter. I wasted no time clarifying my demands as soon as the call connected. My voice was laced with the promise of retribution. "If your organization attempts to harm me again, know that you will feel the full weight of my wrath." A hollow chuckle echoed through the line as the leader sneered back at me. "Watch your back, Pope. There are darker forces at play here than just us mere assassins." "Send your best," I shot back confidently. "I'm tired of dealing with amateurs." And with that, I ended the conversation with her before any more threats could be exchanged. But unease settled in my stomach as her ominous warning lingered in my mind. This would be a battle unlike any I had faced before. For now, unseen forces were waiting to strike against me. But I refused to back down or rest until I emerged victorious, no matter the cost.

As I awoke to another day of potential danger, I strapped on my boots and grabbed my rifle. The sun began peering over the horizon as I set out for my daily perimeter check. My home, a remote fortress nestled among dense trees and jagged cliffs, was constantly under siege by relentless assassins. I inspected every inch of my fence and security systems, double-checking that they were armed and ready to alert me at the slightest hint of intrusion. But despite my precautions, I couldn't shake the fear that my enemies may have learned about my defenses. I trekked deeper into the woods to counteract this vulnerability, placing hidden surveillance cameras strategically. With each step, I felt the panther-type creature I named Ebony's presence at my side. She was a magnificent wolfhound who had somehow found her way into my life. Her silent companionship gave me strength and courage. Every morning, we ran along the defense line together. Ebony moved effortlessly, her sleek form cutting through the crisp air. We stopped at a weathered boulder overlooking the vast ocean, where Ebony would settle at its base, her amber eyes fixed on me with understanding. As we watched the waves crash against the rocky shore in those quiet moments, I told her, "I am the last of my kind. And perhaps you are the last of yours."Though Ebony could not respond with words, her unwavering gaze seemed to affirm our unspoken bond. Each day, our connection deepened, bridging the isolation gap that once consumed me. Despite the looming threat of danger and uncertainty for the future, I found comfort in Ebony's silent companionship. In those quiet moments atop the weathered boulder, hope glimmered amidst the darkness that threatened to consume me.

Despite the distractions caused by the assassins, my duties as a member of the Star Shipping Company remained my top priority. So, despite all the chaos and uncertainty, I stood firmly on Space Station 50, determined to fulfill my responsibilities. The Admiral's voice was filled with pride as he shared news of our recent successes - an increase in work from the Empire's top three shipping companies, a surge of new clients seeking our services, and an increase in contracts pushing our current fleet's limits. As I listened, I thought maybe it was time to aim higher. With newfound determination, I broached the subject with the Admiral, suggesting we acquire another ship, a mid-size freighter. I outlined my vision for equipping this new addition with state-of-the-art defensive systems, such as laser control and rocket launch capabilities, to navigate the treacherous areas of the Empire. To my satisfaction, the Admiral nodded, acknowledging the need to bolster our arsenal against potential threats. With stubborn determination, I promised to take charge and contact Starship Enterprises to inquire about building our envisioned ship with the necessary equipment for our safety and success.

After consulting with the Assassin's Guild, I realized the importance of preparing for future attacks. So, I took it upon myself to strengthen and fortify my defenses. With my trusty starship, the Little Star, at my disposal, I consulted Allie, its advanced AI system, for guidance. Trusting her vast database, I requested the coordinates of the asteroid that served as the Raiders' home base. Once received, I set a course for our intended destination. As soon as we arrived, I sprang into action. I searched every inch of the base for crates of unregistered missiles, a crucial component of my retaliation strategy. After locating two crates, I quickly pried them open and transferred their contents to my ship, replacing the standard traceable missiles. The satisfaction of obtaining these valuable assets filled me with determination and confidence. Mission accomplished. I returned to Space Station 50. Allie was tasked with erasing evidence of our trip to the asteroid base. There had to be no trace of our activities, so I instructed Allie to fabricate an alternate itinerary to fool any potential investigation. She assured me of her ability to perform this task flawlessly without hesitation. Now equipped with two untraceable missiles in my arsenal, I had a formidable defense against possible assassination attempts. Though I am aware of the questionable nature of my actions, self-preservation is paramount to me. I am determined to persevere until the balance is in my favor.

After two long weeks, the high-pitched wail of my security system pierced the silence of the night, instantly jolting me from my slumber and sending my heart racing. Adrenaline coursed through my veins as I rushed to the security monitor, fear gripping me at the sight of four shadowy figures rapidly approaching my location. They had bypassed my outer defenses, a clear sign of a breach. Cursing myself for not keeping my rifle nearby, I grabbed my concealed laser, grateful to have it always at hand. Sprinting to the top floor, I saw two intruders scaling the building with ropes and hooks while their accomplices stood ready to follow. Just when all hope seemed lost, a blur of movement emerged from the forest's darkness - Ebony, my faithful companion, a large wolf-like animal, charged at the attackers with ferocity and precision. In a matter of seconds, she had dispatched two of them, their demise a brutal and gruesome spectacle that momentarily stunned me. With Ebony's unexpected assistance, I quickly killed the remaining assassins, ensuring that they met the same fate as their comrades. But as relief washed over me, I realized that I couldn't leave the two bodies Ebony had taken down, leaving evidence for anyone to trace this deadly encounter back to Ebony. So, without hesitation, I loaded the bodies into my vehicle and drove to the desolate shores of the beach. As I watched their lifeless forms sink beneath the unforgiving waves, I felt finality. I was grateful for Ebony's unwavering support in my time of need and knew she would always have my back. Once the grim task was complete, I contacted the authorities and informed them of what had happened and where they could find the two bodies. It wasn't an easy decision, but necessary for our safety and survival.

The team responsible for the investigation had just arrived to handle the attack's aftermath. The lead investigator, visibly concerned about the situation, expressed his worry, saying, "You're not exactly making allies with the Assassin's Guild." In response, Pope, feeling the weight of the predicament, replied, "I understand that, but what choice do I have? Should I just let them kill me?" Understanding the gravity of the situation, the chief investigator admitted, "I know it's not ideal, but unfortunately, I see no other way to stop them. All I can do is advise you to remain vigilant, as I believe their attempts to harm you will continue." Pope tried to reassure himself and the investigator, saying, "Don't worry, I'll be on my guard." Determined to protect his new family and take action against the Assassin's Guild, he was ready to face the inevitable consequences.

As evening fell and the investigation team left, it was time for us to rest. But before we could retire for the night, a faint scratching sound at the door caught my attention. My thoughts immediately returned to our recent encounter with the assassins, and I wondered if Ebony, our faithful animal companion, was outside. Cautiously, I opened the door and saw Ebony looking up at me pleadingly. Caught in a dilemma, I weighed the risks of letting her in against the potential danger she could bring. But I couldn't shake the memory of her bravery in protecting us. Turning to my adopted sisters, I sought their counsel, asking if they were too afraid or trusted my judgment. Their vote of confidence encouraged me, and with a nod, I beckoned Ebony into the safety of our home. As she stepped inside, I could feel the collective relief in the room. Ebony sat gracefully and exuded a sense of belonging as my sisters tentatively reached out to offer her affection. She accepted their gestures with ease in the warmth of their welcome. Curious about her sudden desire to join us in the house, my sisters asked questions. Reflecting on her behavior, I explained that perhaps Ebony, like many creatures, sought the companionship of a pack and found security in our midst.

As the night went on, it was finally time to rest after a long and eventful day. I led Ebony to my bedroom, grateful for her constant presence by my side. I set up a makeshift bed of oversized blankets at my foot. I couldn't help but smile as Ebony settled in comfortably. She had become more than just a protector; she was now an integral part of our growing family. As we drifted to sleep, I wondered what the new day would bring and was excited to see how our dynamic would change. The next morning, as I prepared for the day ahead, I received an urgent call from the Admiral. He informed me of an outbreak of X-35 Fever on the planet Taxore and the need for immediate vaccine delivery. However, their freighters were unavailable, and she needed my starship to transport them. Without hesitation, I agreed to take on the task.

This mission represented a pivotal moment for me. It provided the opportunity to bring an end to the threat posed by the Assassin's Guild, an organization that had been endangering the lives of my loved ones. I calculatedly decided to use the mission as a guise for engaging the guild, fully aware of the risks involved. It would be challenging if I failed and could not vindicate myself from their accusations. Despite the weighty moral implications of my actions, my unwavering priority has always been the protection of those closest to me. It was a gamble I was prepared to take, even if it meant bearing the burden of guilt and the strain of deception in the coming days.

As I arrived at Station 50 with my trusted ally, Ally, we were tasked with a vital mission – delivering life-saving vaccines to the planet Taxore and launching a decisive strike at the heart of the dangerous Assassin's Guild on the planet Ikxor. We loaded the essential vaccines onto my ship with precision and efficiency before I replaced our missiles with untraceable ones sourced from the Raider's asteroid. The daring move was necessary to safeguard myself and my family from the relentless assassins. With the new missiles securely in place, we charted our course towards the planet Iketer, resolute in our determination to identify and eradicate the Assassin's Guild headquarters. Our honed reconnaissance skills proved invaluable as we pinpointed their heavily fortified compound as we approached the planet. Without hesitation, I locked on to the target and deployed the Raider's missiles, obliterating the stronghold.

With a deep sense of relief, I knew our mission was far from over. Our crucial task was to deliver the life-saving vaccines and ensure their swift arrival at their intended destination. Equipped with our state-of-the-art star drive, we were able to traverse space at unparalleled speeds, making our journey remarkably efficient. To evade detection by potential adversaries, we employed cutting-edge experimental technology to cloak our movements and obscure our actions. Upon our return to our base, I strategized with Allie, my invaluable AI companion. We needed to meticulously erase all traces of our involvement in the decimation of the Assassin's Guild compound. We devised a meticulous plan for Allie to create a backup cube containing all our mission records. Once the backup was complete, I would subtly substitute my current cube with this one before docking at Station 50. This precautionary measure would guarantee that even if an investigative team awaited us upon our arrival, they would uncover no evidence linking us to the attack on the Assassins.

As Allie assured me everything would be in place upon our arrival, I felt relief and gratitude for having such a capable AI by my side. Our calculated risks had paid off, and I was confident that we could proceed with our operations without interference from the Assassins. As our ship docked at the station, my instincts about the Empire police waiting for me were proven correct.

The Empire Police were eagerly awaiting our arrival. The Chief Investigator and her team of experts immediately began their investigation. She approached Commander Pope with disturbing news: the Assassin's compound had been attacked and destroyed, and he was considered a prime suspect. The investigators requested permission to comb my ship for evidence, which Commander Pope granted after understanding the gravity of the situation. I assured the lead investigator that I would cooperate fully with the investigation, and they expressed interest in accessing the AI cube for data on our recent voyage. They planned to investigate the designated area of the ship where the missiles used in the attack were believed to have been launched.

The technician extracted and analyzed data from the AI cube, confirming no deviations or potential trips to the planet where the attack occurred. The investigation then moved to the missiles themselves, with a representative from the starship manufacturer confirming that their serial numbers matched those installed before the test run. Despite thorough investigation, the investigators deemed it impossible to determine whether this ship's missiles had been launched. This was because two dummy missiles were also fired during the test run, making distinguishing between real and false launches difficult. With this information, the lead investigator cleared Commander Pope of any suspicion and closed the case. I breathed a sigh of relief that everything had gone as expected and informed the Admiral that we had completed our mission. After reporting to the Admiral at the shipping office, I left feeling relieved that we had delivered the vaccines without a hitch.

Chapter 10

With my spaceship fully equipped and ready to go, I feel the pull to return to Earth. Despite the discomfort of revisiting memories, I am drawn back home for a brief respite. Stepping into my newly acquired starship, I initiate a conversation with my trusted AI companion, Allie, whose voice reminds me of a female presence. "Allie," I address her, "I need you to retrieve the coordinates of Earth from the fleet database. We are setting a course for my home planet." To my surprise, Allie quickly retrieves the necessary information, taking only a few minutes to locate Earth in the vastness of space. She outlines our route, which involves traveling through three wormholes to reach our destination. With our star drive operating at an impressive 80% efficiency, she estimates our travel time at approximately 7-10 days due to its enhanced performance.

As I planned our journey, I tasked Allie with arranging the necessary supplies for our round trip. With everything in place, I have set a departure date for two days from now and mentally prepared myself for what awaits me on Earth. I am grateful for Allie's well-intentioned advice and thank her, where preparations for the journey home await me. The weight of her words hangs in the air, reminding me of the dangers that await me upon my arrival. However, fueled by determination and a longing to reconnect with my past, I steel myself for the challenges ahead as we set course for the remnants of a world scarred by the Roton attack. As my ship glides through space toward Earth, I cannot contain my excitement. Memories of my childhood and the comfort of familiar landscapes flood my mind, and I can't wait to be back on my home planet. But just as the outline of Earth's star system comes into view, my AI companion Allie interrupts with an urgent voice. "Captain, I've detected an alien ship orbiting Earth. Its intentions are unknown." My heart sinks at the news. I must confront this threat before it can harm Earth or myself. Determined, I steer my ship closer to investigate. As we approach the alien vessel, alarms blare through the cockpit. The ship is heavily armed, and its intentions are still unclear. But I can't turn back now. I have to protect my home and everything I hold dear.

I took a deep breath and steeled my nerves for the upcoming battle. "Allie, make sure our weapons are ready," I ordered as we approached the unknown ship and prepared to defend Earth from further harm. I entered the laser-firing pod and positioned myself to engage the Rotons or any other threat ahead. Adrenaline coursed through my veins as we approached the mysterious ship, my mind racing about who or what might be behind it. The sleek silhouette of the ship came into view against the vastness of space, sending a shiver down my spine. Tension rose on board as we prepared for the inevitable collision. "We're in range, Captain," Allie's voice was calm, but I could feel the gravity of the situation weighing heavily on her. The ship vibrated beneath my feet as our targeting system locked onto the intruder. I gripped the control panel, my knuckles turning white with tension as I gave the order to fire. A bright burst of energy erupted from the ship's laser, sending a volley of fiery beams at the enemy ship with deadly precision. The explosions lit up the darkness of space, casting long shadows on our faces as we watched with relief, knowing that Earth was safe from harm, at least for now.

After securing the area, I instructed Allie to return to the surface. My heart was heavy, knowing this battle was part of a larger war against unknown adversaries. As our ship descended toward our home planet, I couldn't help but think about the challenges ahead on our journey.

However, I pushed those thoughts aside and focused on the immediate task: returning to Earth and confronting whatever trials awaited us. Upon landing at a concealed location, I spotted a nearby shuttle that seemed to have come from the Roton ship. The dense forest teemed with towering trees and echoing animal calls. With his M35 tightly gripped, John Pope silently walked forward to carry out his vengeful mission. To John Pope, the forest was more than just a beautiful landscape; it was a battleground, a blank canvas on which he sought revenge for the horrors inflicted upon his home planet, Earth. The relentless assault of the Rotonn aliens remained a searing wound in his mind, driving his determination to make them pay for their atrocities. As I maneuvered through the thick foliage, The memories of the Rotonn's destruction consumed him, igniting a fiery rage that propelled him toward his ultimate goal: seeking justice for his people.

John's boots crunched against the fallen leaves as he moved through the dense forest, his rifle clutched tightly in his hands. His eyes were alert, and his senses heightened, ready for any sign of danger. Suddenly, a low rustling sound from the underbrush brought him to a halt, his grip on the weapon tightening. A group of Roatan aliens emerged from the dense foliage, their grotesque four-eyed heads sending a shiver down his spine. Without hesitation, John raised his M35 rifle and aimed it at the approaching Roton. He squeezed the trigger with practiced precision, the sound of gunfire echoing through the dense forest. Each shot hit its target with deadly accuracy. The aliens did not match John's determination and expert marksmanship despite their advanced technology. As the last of them fell to the forest floor, John stood amidst the aftermath, his chest heaving with exhaustion and pride. He knew that with each enemy defeated, Earth was one step closer to healing from their devastation. With grim determination, John continued his solitary journey through the forest, ever vigilant for any remaining threats.

He was determined to protect Earth from those who sought to harm it, no matter how long it took. Walking through the shadows toward the shuttle bay, he encountered a lone guard, whom he swiftly and silently eliminated. Approaching the shuttle, he was heartbroken to discover two large dogs lying lifeless on the ground, their bodies mangled by the relentless alien attack. Anger and grief washed over him as he knelt beside them, muttering bitterly, "They never cease their violence, do they?" It was a stark reminder of the ruthless nature of the aliens. As time seemed to stretch endlessly, he remained determined to defend his planet from any threat. Safeguarding Earth was his unwavering purpose, and he was committed to his duty without hesitation. Moving soundlessly through the darkness toward the shuttle bay, he encountered a solitary guard who stood watch with his gaze fixed on the distant horizon. Swiftly and efficiently, he dispatched the guard and pressed on toward his objective. The shuttle stood imposingly before him, its metallic surface glistening faintly in the light of the distant alien moons. However, as he approached, a wave of despair swept over him at the grim scene that unfolded - two large dogs lay motionless on the ground, their bodies ravaged by the relentless onslaught of the alien attackers. A surge of anger and sorrow engulfed him as he knelt beside them. "Their violence knows no end, does it?" he murmured bitterly, once more confronted by the ruthless nature of the alien aggressors.

Determined to complete his mission, he sabotaged the shuttle with practiced efficiency. But just as he turned to leave, a faint sound in the eerie silence of the alien-infested terrain caught his attention. A barely audible whimper came from the thick foliage nearby. Intrigued yet cautious, he approached the source of the sound and slowly parted the dense undergrowth to reveal a heartbreaking sight. Two small pups, orphaned and vulnerable, looked up at him with pleading eyes. Their innocence tugged at his heartstrings, stirring a pang of compassion. What should I do?" he pondered, torn between his duty and humanity.

It was inconceivable to him to leave these helpless creatures to fend for themselves in this harsh world. With a resolute decision, he scooped the pups into his arms, their trust in him evident in their gentle nuzzling against his chest. "I cannot abandon them," he said as he returned to his landing site.

And so began a new journey for him, guided not only by duty but also by compassion and empathy for these innocent creatures. "I will protect you," he whispered to the cubs as they began their journey together. As he continued his journey, a silent promise echoed in his heart - to protect the defenseless from the unrelenting darkness. With two small lives clutched to his chest, he pressed forward into an uncertain future, guided by compassion amidst the shadows of war. After taking in the sights and sounds of his homeworld, it was time for John Pope to return to the Empire. Returning from his relentless mission against the Roatan aliens, John returned to his homeworld's familiar yet changed landscape. Though scars of destruction still marred the once-thriving Earth, a glimmer of hope lingered in the air. Taking a few days to reconnect with the world he had fought so hard to protect, John allowed himself moments of peace amidst the ruins of his past. Memories of better times intertwined with echoes of recent battles offered him brief moments of solace.

After a short break, John returned to the Empire to resume his duties as a partner in the shipping company. This time, he wasn't alone; he had two puppies at his side, who had been rescued from a grim fate by the Pope. As he looked into their innocent eyes, I gathered supplies and set up a safe pen for my little companions on board before I left. It wouldn't be safe for them to roam freely around the ship. With that taken care of, I turned my attention to preparing a meal from the ship's supplies. After whipping up a makeshift meal, I watched intently as the puppies sniffed at it before eagerly digging in. Hopefully, their stomachs will agree with this meal. I think about Ebony and how she might view our new additions as potential snacks. I'll deal with misunderstandings when we get home, but take it as it comes. They traveled back to the Empire together, their spirits lifted by the bonds of camaraderie forged in the chaos of war. As they traveled through the vastness of space, they found comfort in each other's presence, sharing tales of triumph and struggle and envisioning a future where peace and prosperity once again reigned. As they approached the Empire, John felt a sense of excitement building within him. With his newfound allies, he knew that no challenge was too great, no enemy too formidable.

Upon docking at the station, I immediately arranged for a shuttle to take me and my puppies home. As we stepped into our cozy home, we were immediately greeted by my two adopted sisters. Their eyes filled with excitement and joy as they saw the cute little newcomers in our midst. They instantly fell in love with the puppies and showered them with affection, and the anticipation hung heavy as we waited to see Ebony's reaction to the two new additions to our family. I couldn't help but hold my breath, anxious to see how she would react. To my amazement and relief, Ebony welcomed the puppies with open arms - figuratively speaking. She approached them with gentle curiosity, her tail wagging with tentative joy. And to my amazement, the puppies immediately gravitated to her, as if they knew she was their protector and nurturer. As Ebony walked around the house, exploring every nook and cranny, the two puppies followed close behind like obedient shadows. Their bond was palpable with every step, which seemed unbreakable. And when Ebony settled down, they wasted no time snuggling up to her, finding comfort and security in her presence. At that moment, it felt like our little family had grown again. Adding these two furry bundles brought our home an indescribable warmth and joy. As I watched Ebony with her new companions, I found comfort in knowing I now had two more loyal protectors by my side. The two lively and curious puppies now answered to the names of Luna and Cosmo. Their playful antics filled our household with laughter and warmth, their growing presence filling our hearts with unexplainable joy.

Each day, they became more than just pets; they became cherished family members, their wagging tails and wet noses a constant source of comfort and companionship. Once a lone wolf, Ebony took on the role of protector and mentor to the young pups, using her keen instincts and wisdom to guide them through the wonders and complexities of the world. Under her watchful eye, Luna and Cosmo thrived, learning to face life's challenges with courage and resilience. As for me, I resumed my duties within the Empire, balancing my responsibilities with the joys of home life. With Luna and Cosmo by my side, I felt a renewed sense of purpose, knowing that no matter what obstacles lay ahead, I had a loyal family by my side every step of the way. As the years passed, our bond strengthened, fortified by shared experiences and unwavering devotion. Together, we faced life's trials and tribulations with steadfast courage and determination, drawing strength from each other even in the darkest moments. And so, surrounded by the unconditional love of my loved ones and the unwavering loyalty of my companions, I embarked on a new chapter of my life filled with endless possibilities and boundless hope for the future. In the embrace of those we hold dear, we find comfort and inspiration to overcome any challenge that may come our way. As the sun set on another day, casting a warm glow over our home, I couldn't help but feel grateful for the blessings surrounding me. As I settled down for the night, with Luna and Cosmo curled up at my feet and Ebony standing guard by my side, I knew that no matter what tomorrow brought, we would face it together as a family united in love and purpose.

Chapter 11

After returning from my trip to Earth, I resumed my duties at Station 50, working with the Admiral. Our company continues to thrive, and the Admiral believes it is time for us to acquire another mid-size starship. I wholeheartedly agree, especially since we have a backlog of cargo waiting to be shipped. However, I suggest this new ship have a laser firing control system and a missile bay. These additions will allow us to accept shipments bound for dangerous regions of the Empire and ensure their protection from potential raiders. The Admiral has given his approval, and I will contact Starship Enterprises Company to inquire about their ability to build such a specialized ship. After contacting Altaria, the owner of Starship Enterprises, she invited me to her apartment for dinner to discuss the details. We agreed to meet at a local restaurant around 6:30 p.m. During our meeting, we discussed the need for this particular type of ship, and Altaria decided to build it for us. She promised to inform us of her production schedule and estimated completion date. Afterward, we returned to her apartment for evening entertainment and to rekindle our relationship.

. The next day, I left her apartment and returned to my office at the station. To my surprise, I received a phone call from the High Priestess of the Church of Faith. She urged me to call her when I arrived at the office. Without hesitation, I dialed her number and inquired how to help her. To my astonishment, she confided that she needed transportation to the planet Coth0rix for herself and her guard, as her church members had fallen victim to a group of bandits. Sympathetic to her plight, I readily agreed to help. However, I needed to know the size of her party, as my vehicle could only hold a maximum of eight people. With relief, she informed me that she and six of her loyal guards would need transportation. I asked her to give me her current location. I assured her I would pick up her group and promised to let her know the exact time of my arrival. Eager to assist the High Priestess, I felt compelled to inform the Admiral of my intentions. Grateful for my willingness to help, he expressed his gratitude and emphasized the importance of my role within the company. He urged me to exercise caution and be aware of the risks involved.

As I prepared to retrieve the High Priestess and her guard, I consulted our AI assistant to confirm the details of our upcoming journey. To my dismay, the AI informed me that the planet we were heading to was off-limits due to scattered space mines, making any unauthorized landing attempts risky. Worried that this might be a trap, I immediately called the High Priestess, who replied, "Hi, John, what's going on?" Without hesitation, I expressed my concern about their desired destination's dangerous situation and questioned if it was a trap. The High Priestess assured me it was not a trap but an archaeological site that the Empress had reserved exclusively for her church. She apologized for not informing me of the access code necessary for a safe landing and departure from the planet and promised to provide me with the code. With the code in hand, we began our journey, expecting to arrive at our destination in 28 hours.

We quickly navigated through a dangerous minefield when we arrived at the planet. Our landing went smoothly, and we picked up the High Priestess and her six guards without a hitch. Despite the limited space on my ship, we could accommodate them all. It was a pleasant reunion with the High Priestess, whom I hadn't seen since our last encounter. As we talked, I asked about the readiness of her guards for a possible hostage situation. She assured me they were retired soldiers from the 59th Regiment and reminded me that I was an honorary colonel. Confident in their training and abilities, I expressed my satisfaction and discussed the length of our trip. The High Priestess voiced concern about the estimated time frame, recalling that her previous voyage had taken longer than expected. I reassured her that my ship was faster than others thanks to its upgraded star drive, allowing us to travel at a remarkable 135% faster speed than standard drives. Combined with the assistance of my AI ally, we could reach our destination quickly and safely while keeping our advanced technology a secret.

As John Pope and the High Priestess of the Church of Faith, flanked by their guards, approached the distant planet on the viewscreen, they could see their mission. The objective was clear: rescue the Church members being held captive by a mysterious group. Upon landing, they acted quickly, using their training to analyze the situation. The local authorities, who had been struggling to negotiate with the kidnappers, met them on arrival. Once permission was granted, John Pope and the High Priestess took charge of the delicate negotiations. Their primary focus was to establish communication with the kidnappers, understand their motives, and find a peaceful resolution. However, they were also prepared for the possibility of violence, with a plan in place to protect the hostages if talks turned sour. When they reached the building where the meeting was held, tensions were high between the two parties. However, John Pope's calm demeanor and determination helped ease the stress and open channels for meaningful dialogue. The two parties sat and talked for endless hours, delving into every detail, searching for clues or common ground. With each passing second, a thin thread of trust began to weave between them as they worked toward a common understanding. And then, finally, we made a significant breakthrough. The kidnappers finally agreed to release their hostages unharmed in exchange for safe passage off the planet. It was a good, hard-won victory in light of the lingering mystery behind the abduction. As John Pope watched the kidnappers depart and the hostages reunite with their loved ones, he couldn't help but feel an overwhelming sense of relief. They had done their duty to protect the innocent without resorting to violence - something he was proud of. But as they prepared to leave the planet and return home, he couldn't shake the nagging feeling of uncertainty that lingered in the air. What were their true motives?

Pope and the High Priestess were on their way back to Station 50, discussing the reason for their return. The High Priestess mentioned a meeting with the Empress on Guliten Prime, emphasizing its importance. Pope's curiosity remained, and he couldn't help but wonder about her plans after the meeting. "When you're done with the Empress, would you like to stay with me for a few days?" Pope asked hopefully. The High Priestess took a moment to think before answering diplomatically. She appreciated the offer of hospitality, but her schedule was uncertain. "I will let you know. Thank you for the invitation," she replied graciously. Despite the lack of a definitive answer, Pope remained optimistic and looked forward to spending more time with the High Priestess at Station 50. As they traveled, both pondered the possibilities that awaited them upon their return.

After her intense meeting with the Empress, the High Priestess sought refuge in the Pope's secluded home. As she walked through the door, two young women greeted her with a look of astonishment known for her wild, curly hair and mischievous smile, leaning close to her sister Nely and whispering excitedly about the privilege of having the High Priestess as their guest. But amidst the warm greetings and introductions, another household member remained hidden. Ebony, a wolf-like creature with midnight fur and piercing amber eyes, emerged from the shadows. She swatched the group intently, her instincts always on alert as she was a guardian for Pope and his sisters. Pope explained their unique friendship with Ebony to the High Priestess and asked for her discretion in keeping their secret safe. As the High Priestess embraced Ebony, she could sense their deep bond and promised to keep their secret safe with her. Pope thanked her gratefully, knowing she would keep their secret.

John Pope and the High Priestess have just completed a pleasant stay. They are returning to the desert planet where the High Priestess' Church of Faith conducts an extensive archaeological dig. The Empire has provided significant financial support for this endeavor. It is believed that this ancient race possessed technology far beyond what the current Empire possesses. And that this discovery could greatly benefit the Empire or potentially bring disaster. As they descend to the arid planet, John can't help but marvel at the vastness of the landscape, dotted with towering dunes and ancient ruins. Heat radiates from the sand, stinging his skin under his traveling suit. The High Priestess and her entourage quickly make their way to their campsite, leaving John alone with his thoughts. He wonders what wondrous artifacts might be buried beneath the sand, waiting to be unearthed by skilled archeologists. But he also can't shake a nagging sense of foreboding. What if this advanced race had left behind weapons of destruction? Or worse, what if these relics fall into the wrong hands? Despite these concerns, John knows that whatever they find will profoundly affect the Empire. Pope is determined to ensure it will be used for the greater good. Only time will tell what secrets lie buried beneath the desert's unforgiving sands.

Upon returning home, Pope found comfort in the familiar surroundings and the warm embrace of his sisters. He was also comforted by Ebony's presence; they were as close as family, bound by blood and shared experiences. Pope threw himself into his work at Station 50 as the days passed and turned into weeks. Still, his mind often wandered back to the High Priestess's visit and the intrigue it brought. Something about her piqued his curiosity, a desire to unravel her secrets. However, Pope struggled to fulfill his duties and satisfy his thirst for answers during a hectic schedule and responsibilities. He understood that in a world where secrets held power, some truths were best kept hidden, protected by trusted companions and cherished memories. As he contemplated what lay ahead, Pope couldn't help but wonder what adventures, challenges, and discoveries awaited him in the future. As the days passed, Pope immersed himself in the routine of station life, but his thoughts often drifted back to the High Priestess and the secrets she carried. He couldn't shake the feeling that there was more to her story, more to uncover beneath the surface.

Driven by his insatiable curiosity, Pope delved deeper into the Empire's archives, desperately searching for clues to the High Priestess' past and the circumstances that led her to seek his help. But the more he searched, the more the answers seemed to slip through his fingers. Growing increasingly frustrated, Pope sought the counsel of his trusted companions, and they spent countless hours dissecting and analyzing the High Priestess.'

But as the days stretched into long, weary weeks, and the weeks stretched into months, Pope's insatiable quest for answers seemed to lead him deeper into a vast and uncharted territory. And yet, despite the seemingly endless expanse of challenges and obstacles ahead, he remained steadfast in his pursuit of the truth, determined to unravel the mysteries that had consumed his mind and captured his heart. In an ever-expanding universe teeming with mystery and uncertainty, Pope understood that it was often the most daring and risky adventures that tested the limits of courage and curiosity, leading to discoveries that would forever shape history. As he embarked on his journey into the unknown, he knew that whatever dangers and difficulties lay ahead, he would face them with unyielding determination and the unwavering support of those who stood by his side.

Chapter 12

As I entered the palace, I could sense the urgency in the atmosphere. Fleet Admiral Alara and Empress Lysandra stood at the front of the room with grave expressions on their faces, signaling the importance of this meeting. The Fleet Admiral's commanding presence immediately caught our attention as she addressed us. It was clear that something important had happened. In a grave tone, she explained the dire situation that had unfolded: both her esteemed survey ship 25 and the mighty destroyer 41 had been attacked in the far reaches of the Empire. The weight of concern was evident in her voice, leaving no doubt about the gravity of the situation.

As he struggled to process the magnitude of the situation, my mind raced with thoughts, each more urgent than the last. The uncharted territories beyond the reach of our Empire loomed in my mind, a vast expanse of unknown dangers that could threaten our safety and stability at any moment. The Fleet Admiral's revelation only heightened our vulnerability as we learned of the attacker emerging from a mysterious wormhole and its advanced drones mapping our territory. The ship responsible for the devastation was unlike anything we had encountered before; its sleek design and advanced weaponry made us question our defenses and readiness for such threats. As Pope's voice echoed through the conference room, his tone heavy with urgency and determination, I couldn't help but feel a sense of unease settle in my stomach. "What do we do now?" Pope asked, his words heavy with concern and the weight of responsibility. His question hung in the air, underscoring the gravity of the situation and the need for strategic action to protect our Empire. The uncertainty and tension in his tone only added to the sense of urgency, underscoring the importance of making informed decisions to ensure our safety.

As the Empress' voice echoed through the halls, she could feel the weight of her words hanging in the air. The gravity of the situation was present, and every member of the Council felt it in their bones. "To truly grasp the significance of this danger," she spoke with conviction, "we need the expertise of Commander Pope, our laser control officer on my light cruiser. He will investigate this anomaly, identify the attacker, and eliminate the threat." Pope stood tall and determined, his sense of duty driving him forward. He knew that the fate of the Empire rested on his shoulders, and he was determined to complete his mission. When the Fleet Admiral gave the order to leave immediately, a sense of urgency and determination was felt by all present. Commander Pope acknowledged his orders with a crisp salute and turned to face his team. Thoughts raced through his mind about facing the Rotens and this new enemy they had yet to identify. It seemed like one challenge after another, but he wasted no time informing Astra, his partner in the shipping company, of his mission. After making all the necessary arrangements, he prepared to leave and face whatever lay ahead - a daunting task for which he was ready. The rush of duty coursed through his veins as he mentally prepared himself for what was to come.

As I stepped aboard the fleet's light cruiser, my mind raced with anticipation and anxiety. The mission before us was crucial, and our success could shape the future of space exploration. But before I could even catch my breath, I was summoned to the conference room to meet with the captain and commander of the damaged heavy cruiser. Reports indicated that unknown assailants had attacked the wormhole exit. Our ship was on a data-gathering mission with drones when everything went wrong. We lost contact with one of our drones and quickly sent another to assess the situation. A small starship emerged from the wormhole and launched a surprise attack on our ships. The enemy ship moved quickly and with deadly precision, taking out both destroyer escorts in seconds before we could adequately defend ourselves. In a desperate attempt to retaliate, we fired four missiles at their ship while they simultaneously fired two missiles at us. But our weapons were no match for their heavily armored and superior capabilities, as evidenced by the minimal damage inflicted despite our best efforts.

The enemy missiles crashed into our fleet, leaving a trail of smoke and flame in their wake. The impact rocked our ship violently, causing alarm as we scrambled to assess the damage. On the ship's main screen, we watched in horror as the enemy ship disappeared into a swirling wormhole, their escape confirmed. We limped back to Space Station 50, our once-proud starship now a shell of its former self, riddled with gaping holes and scorch marks. As we debriefed with other crew members, it became clear that this was no ordinary enemy. The enemy vessel that had ambushed us was armed with state-of-the-art weapons and formidable attack capabilities, making it a formidable foe.

The thought of facing their full-sized warships filled us with fear and trepidation. In the heavy silence that followed, we couldn't help but ponder the daunting decisions before us as we faced this mighty adversary. The weight of the situation hung heavily in the air, reminding us of the hard road ahead as we prepared to face this powerful enemy.

As we gathered in the war room, voices rose and fell in heated debate. Who were these attackers? Why were they targeting our fleet? Fear gripped us as we considered the possibilities: rival factions seeking control of uncharted territories or aliens from distant galaxies with unknown motives. But one thing was sure - we could not afford to underestimate our enemy. Our survival, and that of the entire Empire, depended on every decision we made from this point forward. Our top strategists huddled together, poring over maps and data, brainstorming new defense plans, and gathering intelligence on the enemy's capabilities and intentions. We were determined to be prepared for the inevitable confrontation that lay ahead. The fate of our fleet hung in the balance, and we worked tirelessly, fueled by determination and fear, to ensure our victory and protect our interests. We could not afford to be retaken by surprise.

After much deliberation, the decision was made to address the pressing issue. The possibility of shutting down the wormhole exit weighed heavily on the team's minds. Could it even be done? As they discussed their options, the Admiral's eyes fell on Doctor Hure, a renowned wormhole expert. "Doctor Hure, as our foremost authority on the subject, can you shed any light on the feasibility of closing or obstructing the wormhole exit?" Doctor Hure's response was discouraging. "Based on my extensive research, closing a wormhole exit is beyond our current technological capabilities. They appear impervious to any intervention," Doctor Hure stated somberly.

The group gathered in the Admiral's conference room, their faces grim as they received the latest news. The mission to enter the wormhole had become even more dangerous, with an enemy fleet waiting on the other side. The Admiral's voice echoed through the room as he outlined their next steps. "As part of our preparations," he said, " We have installed special weapons on our cruiser. We will place them inside the wormhole. However, I must stress the utmost secrecy regarding this operation." The consequences of leaking any information from this meeting were grave and clear. With that order, the meeting was adjourned, and everyone returned to their respective ships. As we all left, a weight hung as we silently contemplated the dangerous mission ahead. I boarded the ship and approached the Admiral to learn more about the mysterious weapon. Sensing my curiosity, he motioned for me to step aside, away from eavesdropping ears, and in a calm tone, explained the nature of the weapons: A proximity mine with high explosives would be used to stop the enemy. If that failed, a nuclear device would be our last resort. However, he sternly warned me not to share this information with anyone. "The Empire has a strict policy against the possession of such weapons. They were banned over five centuries ago and have been stored in a secure facility on an abandoned planet for over millennia," he said, stressing the importance of secrecy as he explained the plan to deliver the weapon deep into the wormhole using a drone transport equipped with a proximity detection system. "John, you must not discuss this with anyone," he repeated firmly. I nodded understanding and reassured him, "Don't worry, Admiral. Your secret is safe with me." With determination and a sense of the gravity of our mission, we prepared to embark on this dangerous task while keeping everything shrouded in secrecy. The stakes were high, but we were ready to face whatever challenges lay ahead.

We navigated to the wormhole's exit, our ship flanked by two sleek destroyers. Admiral Thorne's booming commands echoed through the comms system, his heavy cruiser looming protectively behind us. The admiral quickly launched a drone armed with a proximity mine. However, before the mine could be placed in the wormhole, a small enemy ship emerged. Without warning, it fired two missiles at us. I immediately activated our laser defense system and successfully intercepted both missiles. In response, I aimed our lasers at the enemy ship, but my first two shots caused only minor damage. Frustrated, I targeted the rear of their ship, where their star drive was located. With a satisfying explosion, their ship shattered into countless fragments and disappeared. As the adrenaline began to wear off, I couldn't help but feel a sense of familiarity. A distant memory tugged at my mind, but I couldn't quite place it. There was a slight delay after my laser strike before the ship was destroyed.

We stood at the wormhole's entrance in tense anticipation, fingers hovering over buttons and screens. Pope's hand shook slightly as he gripped the control panel, his eyes never leaving the other end of the swirling vortex. The hours of waiting were finally over when we heard a loud explosion from inside the wormhole. Our plan had worked; our trap had been sprung. Excitement and nervous energy crackled in the air as we prepared for the arrival of our target. And sure enough, moments later, a massive ship emerged from the wormhole, casting a dark shadow against the endless expanse of space. Without hesitation, our enemy fired a missile at our cruiser, but John was quicker and shot it down with a well-aimed laser blast. The battlefield fell silent as we faced our crippled enemy, their ship now nothing more than a floating metal carcass with a gaping hole in its side and a destroyed bridge. Our captain's voice cut through the silence like a knife: "John, finish the ship." But instead of obeying the order, John hesitated, his gaze fixed on the damaged ship before us. He saw not a threat but an opportunity. "The ship is already dead," he said calmly to the captain. "But its technology could be valuable to us. I suggest we board it and salvage what we can."

The captain's brow furrowed in concern as he peered through the screens of their spaceship, assessing the damaged enemy vessel floating in front of them. "And what of the enemy crew? Are there any lives aboard?" John's heart raced as he relayed the information from his scans. "I believe the ship is crewless, controlled by advanced AI software. They are probably programmed to self-destruct if damaged, but this one was spared that fate by the unexpected detonation of the mine in the wormhole." With a commanding nod from the Captain, John and his team began preparing to board, checking their weapons and securing their helmets. Adrenaline surged through their bodies as they visualized the potential challenges and dangers that awaited them inside the disabled ship. The air around them crackled with tension and anticipation as they prepared for this dangerous and unpredictable mission.

I made an urgent plea to the Admiral, stressing the urgent need for an expert in explosives and another in electronic software to join me on my mission to infiltrate the disabled enemy ship. The captain promised to seek the admiral's approval before proceeding with my request. Moments later, the Admiral's face appeared on the ship's comm screen, eyes narrowed in concern. After a brief pause, the Admiral confirmed they could provide my team with an electronics and software specialist. However, they also mentioned consulting Baroness Futuris, a renowned explosives and demolition expert from a nearby Empire planet. A wave of relief washed over me at the thought of having such experienced individuals on my side. The Admiral promised me that the two experts would be transported to me via a shuttle without delay.

Along with the specialists, she proposed using two armed drones to aid us in our battle against the enemy vessels. I expressed my gratitude for her unwavering backing and vowed to be ready for the upcoming mission upon the team's arrival. The Admiral guaranteed that she would arrange for the specialists to promptly join me on the shuttle and dispatch two drones to assist us in defeating our foes.

As we approached the damaged ship, its metal hull gleamed in the distant starlight. I could feel the vibration of our shuttle's engines as we prepared for a dangerous journey through the vast emptiness of space. The commander instructed us to prepare for entry, and we quickly secured ourselves to the tether line with our suits sealed tight and our breathing masks in place. The gap between our shuttle and the disabled ship seemed to stretch forever as we crossed it, each step more crucial than the last. My heart raced with excitement and fear as I gazed at the seemingly endless darkness around us. We finally made it inside the ship, and the sight that greeted us was one of utter destruction. The walls were charred and twisted, wires hung loosely from their casings, and debris littered its battered state. She informed us that she was most likely responsible for the ship's failure to self-destruct. As she examined the sophisticated technology before her, I couldn't help but marvel at its advanced capabilities. It far surpassed anything I had encountered in all my years as an investigator. "We need to get this back to our lab for further analysis," I said, nodding in agreement with her assessment. Following the Commander's orders, she carefully secured the equipment in a bag and returned to the shuttle, wary of any lingering danger.

Meanwhile, I checked on our progress with the Baroness. Her sharp eyes scanned every inch of the ship for any remaining explosives, dismantling the units using her extensive knowledge of wireless control systems. With each device neutralized, she calmly reported back to me until only one remained."Once this is taken care of, I'll return to the shuttle," she said, her focus unwavering as she worked to disarm the final explosive. I couldn't help but feel concerned for her safety as I urged her to return to our shuttle's safety. But as always, she remained calm and focused, ensuring our mission was completed before returning to safety.

"I will come with you, Commander," she insisted, her eyes pleading to be by my side as we faced our dangerous mission. But I knew the dangers ahead and couldn't risk putting her in harm's way. "This is my responsibility, Baroness," I said firmly, trying to hide the fear in my voice. "Your orders stand - return to the shuttle and await further instructions." Reluctantly, she nodded and returned to the safety of the shuttle. As she disappeared into the shadows, her unwavering dedication left me with a feeling of admiration. I took a deep breath and turned to face the remaining threat, hoping to defuse the explosive and ensure the success of our mission. The weight of our entire team's safety now rested on my shoulders.

I lifted the charge with a steady hand, feeling its weight pull heavily on my arm. The danger of what I was holding was ever present in my mind as I carefully made my way through the damaged ship. My feet tiptoed delicately over debris and twisted metal, my breath held tightly in my chest. Each step brought me closer to the breach in the hull, the gaping hole beckoning ominously. Determined, I let go of the charge and watched it fall into the abyss below. A moment of silent devotion passed before a violent shockwave erupted around me, knocking me off balance and sending me hurtling across the ship's crumbling interior. I slammed into a jagged wall, a searing pain shooting through my head on impact. Yet I remained conscious amidst the chaos. As I frantically returned to the shuttle, my head throbbed with every movement. Minutes later, it arrived, and I gratefully climbed aboard, ready for a respite from the intense mission. When I reported to the Admiral, he heaved a sigh of relief at our success. I confidently informed him that the ship was secure and ready to be towed back to the safety of the space station. A destroyer was already on its way to ensure a smooth return trip without further complications or dangers lurking in our path.

As my mission duties ended, I turned to my team members - the elegant Baroness and our skilled electronics technician. Our eyes met, a shared sense of unease settling over us at the thought of the new enemy we had encountered and the unknown challenges ahead. With a heavy heart, I ordered them to return to their respective ships. As they departed, I couldn't shake the uncertainty in the air. We found ourselves outnumbered, facing an adversary with superior technology and tactics. As we braced for what was to come, we could only wait for time to reveal our next move. Upon arrival at the nearest inhabited planet, scientists inspected our damaged alien vessel thoroughly. What they discovered inside its battered hull left us all in awe. Despite significant damage from the nearby mines, the material the ship was made of appeared to be unlike anything recorded in the Empire's vast archives. It seemed almost alien in its construction. However, the most significant challenge still lay ahead - deciphering the AI software inside the ship. Its intricate programming held secrets that could potentially change the course of history. As I contemplated this daunting task, I couldn't help but wonder about the enigmatic beings who had created such advanced technology and what they might be capable of.

Upon further analysis, it became apparent that this material possessed unprecedented unheard-of properties in the Empire's territories. The smooth metallic surface shimmered in the sunlight, almost pulsating with a mysterious energy. And the advanced technology built into the ship was unlike anything the Empire had ever seen, its intricate electronic components dwarfing any advancement they knew.

The implications of such a discovery were profound - proof of a civilization far beyond the Empire's reach. As the scientists delved deeper into their research, it became clear that understanding the full extent of this remarkable find would be no easy task. Understanding its vast capabilities would take months of focused study and experimentation.

As they pieced together more information about this powerful enemy, it became increasingly clear that the Empire faced an opponent whose mastery of technology surpassed anything they had encountered. It was a frightening realization that left them vulnerable and uncertain about what lay ahead for their Empire.

A stroke of luck occurred when a series of proximity bombs were strategically placed within the wormhole, successfully disabling the formidable spacecraft of the aliens. Tension filled the air as the advanced society's calculated aggression loomed over them, backed by impressive military prowess. Whispers and speculation abounded as they awaited the harsh reality to set in. Like a ship navigating treacherous waters, the once mighty Empire stood at a crucial crossroads, facing daunting challenges that could determine their fate. Would they rise above them with ingenuity and determination? Only time would tell as they held their breath and braced themselves for whatever came next in these intergalactic battles."

After two long weeks of standing by the imposing wormhole, our orders finally came through from Admiral Vega. We were to return to Goliten Prime aboard the large light cruiser Empress. As soon as we docked at the busy station, I went to the command center to see if we needed a detailed report of our time at the wormhole. To my surprise, the Empress declined, stating that a formal meeting would be held upon Admiral Vega's return. My thoughts immediately turned to home and all the things I couldn't wait to do when I arrived. I missed my puppies terribly and couldn't wait to see how much they had grown since my last visit. And I had an exciting surprise planned for my sisters - a booth at the theater for the upcoming season so they could enjoy all the shows. While I was away, They cared for me and my furry friends, so it was only fitting to show appreciation with this gesture. As we traveled back in the shuttle, my mind was worried about the future. The constant threat of assassins lurked in the back of my mind as I pondered the challenges ahead. With Rotons wreaking havoc and a mysterious new enemy known as "The Strangers" appearing at the wormhole, there was never a dull moment in this chaotic environment. Sometimes, I questioned the wisdom of pushing my luck and risking my life in this dangerous world. But deep down, I knew that only time would reveal the actual outcome of my decisions.

I was summoned to an emergency meeting at the Imperial Palace. The atmosphere in the great hall was tense, with a palpable sense of urgency in the air. Empress Lasre stood at the front, her regal presence commanding attention as she emphasized the gravity of our current situation. Her unwavering determination and sharp words set the tone for what would undoubtedly be a fierce battle ahead.

As we took our seats around the large conference table, Empress Lasre's authoritative voice echoed throughout the chamber. She shared vital information gleaned from the captured enemy ship, emphasizing its importance in uncovering the identity of our new adversary. Our scientists and engineers stationed at the wormhole had made intriguing discoveries that shed light on the mysterious enemy. According to our sophisticated starship AI, there were no physical beings aboard the ship, a puzzling discovery that only deepened the mystery. One circulating hypothesis suggested that we were facing not a tangible enemy but a powerful software adversary with advanced AI capabilities.

But this theory remained unconfirmed, leaving us to grapple with uncertainty and prepare for whatever lay ahead in this intergalactic war.

Meanwhile, the engineers worked tirelessly to study and understand the alien material that made up the captured ship's hull. Despite being hit by multiple laser blasts in an earlier encounter with John, it remained surprisingly undamaged. Pope raised concerns about the enemy's advanced technology - if their ship could withstand such attacks, what chance did they have against their powerful weapons? It became clear that the Empire was facing an elusive and formidable opponent unlike any they had encountered before.

The gravity of the situation led to a unanimous decision: gather more information before devising a plan of action against this unknown threat. After further study of the captured ship, the meeting concluded with an agreement to reconvene. As preparations for battle began, the future of the Empire felt uncertain. With thoughts and questions swirling in their minds about these mysterious adversaries, the attendees left with a renewed determination to confront them head-on. Armed with new knowledge and an unwavering spirit, the Empress and her team prepared for what lay ahead. Due to the gravity of the situation, it was unanimously decided that further information needed to be gathered before devising a plan of action for this unfamiliar danger. The meeting concluded with plans to reconvene after receiving additional information from the ongoing investigation of the captured ship. The fate of the Empire hung in the balance as they prepared to face a mysterious and powerful enemy. The meeting left everyone with lingering questions about their mysterious adversaries: Who were they? Where did they come from? What drove their actions? These questions weighed heavily on our minds and fueled our determination to confront them head-on.

Armed with new knowledge and unwavering resolve, the Empress and her team prepared to take on this new adversary. Before leaving, the Empress approached me and inquired about my availability to return to service for the Empire. I accepted without hesitation, expressing my gratitude for her continued support. She informed me of the upgrades made to her cruiser's laser control system, including new, more powerful generators and the ability to fire both lasers simultaneously from one pod. I promised to schedule a test session once the system was fully operational, and then we could head for the wormhole. The Empress thanked me for my willingness to help and expressed her appreciation.

Chapter 13

The Empress sat regally at the head of the large conference table, her deep brown eyes scanning the faces of those gathered for the emergency meeting. The room was filled with high-ranking officials, including Commander John Pope, four admirals, and ten starship captains, all seated around the massive table. The tension in the air was palpable as they eagerly awaited the Empress' following words, and when she began to speak, her voice rang with authority and determination. "We have a new threat from the other end of the wormhole," she announced, her eyes flashing with concern. "They have launched relentless attacks against our planet, and we must devise a plan to defeat them."The group exchanged worried glances before each offered their scenarios and strategies. But it was Commander Pope who spoke up with a bold proposal. He suggested they form a mission to go through the wormhole and attack their enemy's main planet."It is doubtful that there are any living beings on their planet," he confidently told the group. "A powerful AI system most likely controls it." The others nodded in agreement, seeing the logic in his suggestion. After careful consideration, the Empress gave her approval on one condition: they must confirm that there are no innocent lives on the enemy's home planet before launching an attack. All eyes turned to Admiral Vega and Commander Pope as they were tasked with leading the mission and ensuring its success. The room erupted in excited discussion as plans were made and preparations began. The fate of their existence rested on this crucial mission, and everyone knew it would be a challenging and dangerous journey.

The Admiral and Commander Pope began to form the fleet in preparation for their attack on the AI at the wormhole's other end. The tension was high; they all knew this would be a critical phase in their war against the enemy. The fleet consisted of a heavy cruiser 47, under Commander Pope's command, which would lead the charge and destroy the AI on the adversary's planet. Following closely behind were four light cruisers and 16 destroyers, ready to engage any of the AI's starships within their solar system. As the Admiral informed the captains of their mission, they braced themselves for what would surely be a high casualty rate. But they were all willing to do whatever it takes to protect their empire.

In two weeks, they would converge at the wormhole and attack. With a final command from the Admiral, Commander Pope and his heavy cruiser will lead the way into the unknown, determined to defeat the AI once and for all. As everyone returned to their ships and prepared for battle, the Admiral and Commander Pope sat down to prepare a detailed sequence for their fleet's journey through the wormhole. They knew this was a make-or-break situation for their empire, and failure was not an option.

As the last of the participants left, I pulled Admiral Vega aside to discuss my proposed changes to the plan. My heart raced with determination and fear as I shared my ideas for the mission. The weight of responsibility on my shoulders was almost suffocating, but I knew this was a necessary step to defeat the AI that threatened our Empire. A hush fell over the dimly lit conference room as I spoke. The other officers met my words with tense nods and furrowed brows. My voice grew steadier with each sentence, masking the nerves fluttering in my stomach."I wish to take command of my starship, Little Star," I declared, standing tall even as my hands trembled at my sides. "Along with two of your most powerful nuclear missiles." It was a bold move that could potentially jeopardize any chance of success. But I believed it was our best chance to defeat the AI once and for all. I could feel the weight of everyone's eyes on me as I continued to outline my plan. The burden of responsibility grew with each passing second, threatening to crush me under immense pressure, but I pressed on, determined to see this through. "This could be a suicide mission," I admitted my voice now barely above a whisper. "And I don't want to put the heavy cruiser's crew at risk."My gaze flickered to Admiral Vega, silently pleading for his support. He gave a curt nod, signaling his agreement with my proposal.

Taking a deep breath, I made a final point. "My ship has advanced sensors that can detect any living creature on the AI's planet. It could be the key to our victory - if there were no living beings left on the enemy planet, negotiations would be futile, and we would have no choice but to launch our attack. But it was a risk we were willing to take."I will use the transmission of their commands to locate any potential threats," I explained. "And if necessary, we will launch the nuclear weapons at their central location, annihilating them.

The Admiral listened carefully before answering, his face showing signs of deep thought. "Your plan is dangerous, Pope," he said thoughtfully. "But I understand the reasoning behind it. We must do whatever it takes to protect our empire and loved ones from this evil force." He paused briefly before speaking again, his tone laced with genuine concern. "I pray that you return safely from this mission, but if you don't, I vow to protect your family as if they were my own. It is my duty as Admiral of the Fleet." A wave of gratitude washed over me as I sincerely thanked him for his unwavering support. It was no easy task, but I would face it with determination and courage. And even if it meant sacrificing myself, I knew it was a risk worth taking to defend our people and

I carefully loaded the two powerful nuclear weapons onto the small but technologically advanced LittelStar stationed at Dock 14. My hands trembled slightly as I carefully checked and double-checked their secure straps, fully aware of the devastation they could cause. Before leaving on my mission, I called my sisters to say goodbye and assure them I would return soon. As I said these words, a wave of love and protection for my family washed over me. "I'll be home before you know it," I promised determinedly. After saying goodbye, it was time to join the fleet waiting at the wormhole entrance to the AI system. When we arrived, I strategically positioned myself behind the towering light cruisers and heavily armed destroyers, using their formidable presence as cover until we reached the halfway point through the dangerous AI system. That's when I would break away from the group and head for the planet alone, determined to complete my mission no matter the challenges. Finally, with all preparations complete, the Admiral ordered our fleet to enter the wormhole. I prepared myself for what awaited me on this dangerous and unpredictable journey.

We found ourselves amid a tumultuous battlefield after emerging from the wormhole. The AI solar system was a hive of frantic activity, with enemy ships darting in every direction like rabid hornets fiercely protecting their hive. The sleek, metallic forms of the ships shimmered ominously under the distant starlight while explosions illuminated the dark void as cruisers and destroyers clashed in savage combat. As my ship maneuvered away from the chaos and set a course for the AI's home planet, a mix of trepidation and resolve coursed through me. My sensors swept across the barren planet, revealing no signs of life. It could be our chance for a surprise attack. With my steadfast AI ally monitoring their communications commands, we swiftly homed in on the location of their central command center—a colossal structure looming over the desolate landscape. In a daring and resolute move, I armed two nuclear missiles and launched them straight into the heart of the enemy's stronghold, intent on delivering a decisive blow to their forces once and for all.

The explosions erupted in a blinding flash, engulfing the planet in a fiery inferno that lit up the surrounding space. I frantically maneuvered my ship through the chaos of battle, dodging and weaving through the relentless attacks of the planet's defense system. The blazing roar of laser fire and explosions echoed through the vast emptiness of space, leaving a trail of destruction in its wake. My eyes scanned the battlefield, taking in the carnage and devastation surrounding me. In the distance, I spotted three sleek enemy ships racing toward a wormhole, their advanced AI technology far surpassing our own. Despite the intense heat and pressure, I felt a shiver run down my spine as I realized the gravity of the situation. These three ships held the potential to wreak unimaginable havoc on an unsuspecting world. As my ship groaned under the relentless attack, I knew I couldn't follow them through the wormhole. But as they disappeared into the unknown, a sense of dread gripped me - for the fate of our world now rested on this encounter, and only time would tell what its consequences would be.

It was a victory won at a significant cost - a cost that would not soon be forgotten by those who fought bravely in this epic battle. The fleet and I limped back to our home system, exhausted and battered from the fierce battle. Our victory was bittersweet, for we had lost many ships and comrades. The weight of grief hung heavily over all of us, knowing that we would never see our fallen friends again. When we returned, there were no cheers or celebrations, only a somber mood and thoughts of telling the Empress and the families of those who had perished. Their loss was a heavy burden on our hearts, a reminder of the sacrifices made in war. As soon as I brought the Little Star to a safe and secure docking at Station 50, my heart raced with anticipation. I couldn't wait to see my family again after being away for what felt like forever.

The long journey through the vast unknown had been arduous, but the thought of seeing my sisters again had sustained me through the darkest moments. The moment I entered my home, I was greeted by my sisters, their eyes filled with tears. They had been anxiously following the day's events on the local communication stations, and their emotions overflowed as they hugged me tightly. We were a small but close-knit unit, brought together by the shared experience of loss and the constant threat of danger. As we embraced, I could feel the weight of the past year's struggles slowly lifting from my shoulders. I was grateful that the harrowing ordeal was finally behind us. We had faced the unknown and emerged victorious, a testament to our resilience and love for one another. As we sat around the dinner table catching up on the details of our lives that we had missed, I couldn't help but feel a deep sense of peace and contentment. In those simple moments, surrounded by my family's warmth, I realized the true meaning of home. The Little Star may have taken me to the galaxy's far reaches, but it was here, in the safety and love of my family, that I found my true purpose.

Chapter 14

Nine long months after the defeat of the AI invaders, Pope received an urgent message from the High Priestess of the Church of Faith. She needed to return to Goluten Prime for a crucial meeting with the Empress. Out of a sense of duty, I readily agreed to transport him, and we left the following day. She thanked me. She expressed her excitement at our reunion and the importance of this meeting with the Empress. Before leaving the station, however, I secretly entered coordinates into my AI's system for an ancient planet known for its dark secrets. The journey would take 36 hours, but I had to fulfill my plans. My AI informed me of the length of the trip and reminded me of the importance of this upcoming meeting. I mentally and physically prepared myself for what lay ahead on this mysterious planet.

Pope was on a perilous journey to a distant, abandoned planet. Its surface was coated in layers of dust and debris, making it seem like time had stood still in this lonely world. Here, amid the ruins of a once-great civilization, the high priestess reigned with an aura of reverence and wisdom. She led her loyal followers through the treacherous landscape, their eyes fixed on the horizon in search of ancient knowledge that spanned millennia. They were not mere travelers or explorers but archaeologists delving into the depths of time. In their quest, they sought to unravel long-held mysteries about a race that had long ago vanished from history's pages. This elusive race possessed a technology beyond comprehension - wormholes. These gateways bestowed upon their empire the gift of unparalleled speed, allowing them to traverse vast distances across the infinite expanse of the universe in the blink of an eye. But despite their advanced understanding of these miraculous portals, their origins remained obscurity. The architects behind such incredible power had faded into legend and myth, lost to the sands of time. And so, Pope and his fellow adventurers pressed on, driven by an insatiable thirst for knowledge and secrets waiting to be unraveled amid the ruins of this forgotten world.

Under the guidance of the wise and revered high priestess, the Church of Faith was granted special permission to excavate the ruins of a once-great and powerful ancient city. Their mission was twofold: to unearth artifacts that would enrich the empire's understanding of its past and to uncover the secrets behind the genesis of the mysterious wormholes. The dedicated archaeologists labored tirelessly as they carefully sifted through layer upon layer of history. Each artifact they unearthed was like a puzzle piece, revealing glimpses of a long-forgotten world and showcasing a lost civilization's incredible ingenuity and wisdom. These relics were more than mere curiosities; they held the potential to unlock the universe's most profound mysteries within them. The Church of Faith took great care in cataloging each discovery, preserving them for future generations to study and marvel at. As the high priestess believed in keeping knowledge within their ranks, only select artifacts were shared with museums across the empire, serving as symbols of enlightenment for those fortunate enough to encounter them. The remaining artifacts were sold to esteemed collectors, and their proceeds channeled back into the Church's charitable endeavors that spanned across galaxies, aiding those in need in countless ways.

With each swing of their shovels, the high priestess and her followers unearthed relics that seemed to defy logic. A glowing orb that emitted a soothing hum when touched. A machine with buttons and switches that glowed with an otherworldly light. And among the rubble of forgotten buildings, they found carefully preserved documents filled with equations and diagrams that hinted at lost sciences and advanced technology. As they delved deeper into the ruins, the high priestess could feel the weight of history pressing down on her as if the air was thick with the knowledge of those who had come before. But she was determined, for she believed that the secrets hidden within these ancient ruins held the key to unlocking the mysteries of the universe itself. And so, amidst the dust and debris of an abandoned planet, the high priestess and her followers continued their quest for understanding and the legacy left behind by giants long gone.

The AI's voice crackled through the speaker, notifying me of our descent towards the planet Allie. As we neared the surface, the AI announced that it had located a suitable landing spot. I skillfully maneuvered the spaceship onto the designated area and felt a sense of relief as the craft smoothly touched down. Exiting the vessel, I was greeted by the high priestess, who approached me with open arms. Her deep purple robes flowed gracefully behind her as she pulled me into a warm embrace. "It has been too long," she said with genuine affection. "I am well, thank you for asking. And yourself?" I replied with equal warmth. The high priestess explained that she needed to meet with the Empress on Galiten Prime urgently and requested my assistance with transportation. "There will be three of us traveling: myself and two guards," she added. Understanding the gravity of the situation, I nodded gravely in agreement. "I will make all necessary arrangements for your trip," I assured her. Together, we made our way to the designated landing zone, where I prepared for departure to our next destination – Galiten Prime.

As we prepared to board the ship, a frantic parishioner sprinted towards us, gasping for air. "There's been an accident at the excavation site," she panted. "The backhoe operator is trapped under the sand." We rushed back to the site without hesitation, armed with shovels and determination. The scene before us was chaotic - a massive pile of sand covering a backhoe and its operator. With adrenaline pumping through our veins, we began digging, driven by the urgency to rescue the trapped operator. After 25 grueling minutes, we uncovered the buried backhoe and miraculously found the operator still alive inside the cab. We carefully freed her from the sand's grasp and transported her to a nearby medical facility. A team of skilled professionals immediately emerged, using their expertise to revive and stabilize the operator. As we stood together afterward, reflecting on the intense experience, a sense of relief washed over us, knowing that our efforts had saved a life. Despite facing adversity in the form of shifting sands, our unity and determination prevailed. This ordeal tested our limits and strengthened our bonds as we worked tirelessly to protect each other. And in that moment, we knew that together, we could overcome any challenge thrown our way.

Now that things have calmed down, with the driver recovered and Ally at the helm, John conversed with Solaria, the High Priestess. He was curious about how her church became involved in the archaeological dig on the planet. Solaria explained, "After the empire conducted surveys of the planet, they stumbled upon a spot where structures lay buried beneath the ground. It was suspected to be a potential site of the ancients. The previous Empress contacted us to lead the expedition, knowing we had two top archaeologists within the church. She understood the importance of maintaining secrecy, realizing that disclosing the location could attract unwanted attention from individuals looking to exploit the area. John nodded, understanding the delicate balance of power and secrecy involved. Solaria then shared her reason for visiting the Empires, mentioning that they had sent a camera down into a large chamber, revealing crates and equipment. She proposed adding a contingent of troopers to secure the site."I believe providing troopers is a wise decision," John replied, telling about his encounters with various power groups, including the assassins. "It must have been a harrowing experience for you. "Solaria appreciated his understanding and acknowledged the challenges they faced. They agreed to shift the conversation's focus and enjoy the remainder of their journey back home, leaving behind the weight of their responsibilities for a while.

Upon reaching station 55, I arranged for a shuttle to transport the high priestess to the Empress's castle. As we walked, I suggested she rest at my new residence for a few days and meet my intriguing companions. After meeting with the Empress, she promised to let me know if she would join me at my residence. We said our goodbyes and went our separate ways. When we arrived at station 55, I arranged a shuttle to take the high priestess to the Empress's castle. As we strolled towards our destination, I proposed that she rest at my recently acquired home for a few days and meet my exciting companions. After meeting with the Empress, she agreed to let me know if she would visit my residence. We bid each other farewell and parted ways.

After she met with the Empress, she decided to spend a few days with her. When I brought her to my residence, I introduced her to the new family members. The puppies greeted her affectionately, overwhelming her with their curiosity and where they had come from. We spent the rest of her stay in polite conversation while she rested up for her return trip to the desert planet of the ancients. On the way back, our discussion delved into the far-reaching consequences of these findings, which disrupted the precarious balance of our empire. We were teetering on the edge of chaos, with technology beyond our understanding threatening to overthrow everything we knew. It was a dangerous prospect, like opening Pandora's box, with unknown and potentially devastating repercussions. Our expressions grew somber as we grappled with the gravity of our conversation, fully aware of the weight of knowledge we now possessed. The fate of entire worlds hung in the balance. I felt uneasy as we went to Space Station 50 to return to the ancient planet. The archaeological dig had unearthed more than just artifacts; it revealed a truth that would reshape empires and civilizations. And as our ship returned to the site, I couldn't help but wonder what awaited us.

Commander John Pope stood alongside the High Priestess, her regal demeanor and flowing robes marking her as a spiritual leader. Both had recently returned to the planet, marking a pivotal moment in the ongoing archaeological efforts. With their sun-kissed skin and sweat-drenched clothes, the dig team worked diligently to uncover the secrets hidden beneath the surface of the desert planet. Their efforts had unveiled a monumental chamber, its entrance guarded by ancient symbols that spoke of a long-lost civilization. As they excavated deeper into the earth, each layer revealed more mysteries waiting to be discovered.

Now fully excavated, the chamber waited in silence for the arrival and guidance of the High Priestess. Anticipation crackled through the air as team members eagerly awaited her arrival. They knew that with her guidance, they could unlock the secrets within. This recent development underscored the cooperation of the Pope and the Highpreste unfolding narrative of exploration and discovery on the planet. The coming together of these two powerful leaders promised new insights and a possible unraveling of ancient mysteries concealed within the chamber's depths.

The team buzzed with excitement and nervous energy as they prepared for what was to come under the direction of their esteemed leaders. The next few days were poised to be transformative as they delved deeper into the unknown. The team buzzed with excitement and nervous energy as they prepared for what was to come under the direction of their esteemed leaders. The next few days were poised to be transformative as they delved deeper into the unknown, guided by strength and spirituality. Commander John Pope stood at the chamber entrance, his fingers nervously tapping against the ancient stone. He glanced at the High Priestess, adorned in white ceremonial robes and a golden headdress. They exchanged a look of determination as they prepared to open the chamber doors. But just as they were about to push them open, Commander Pope's sharp military instincts kicked in. He remembered reading about archaeologists back on his planet suffering from inhaling the ancient dust within some of the tombs of Egypt. He turned to the team behind him and said, "Wait. We need to take precautions before entering." He explained his concerns about inhaling ancient dust and proposed that they all wear protective masks.

The team quickly followed his lead, donning masks from their backpacks and securing them tightly around their faces. With this crucial adjustment, they were ready to enter the chamber with enhanced safety and preparedness. This moment showcased Commander Pope's dedication to the well-being of his team, which was evident throughout their archaeological endeavors. His decision to implement safety measures reflected his military pragmatism and scholarly caution, highlighting their approach's perfect blend of practical experience and historical knowledge. As they waited for everyone to be geared up, excitement and anticipation grew for what awaited them beyond those ancient chamber doors. Armed with their masks and curiosity, they were ready to uncover the mysteries concealed within.

As the Pope and High Ptestess and their team entered the chamber, they were immediately greeted by several unexpected sights. The first section resembled a maintenance area, with tools and equipment scattered about, hinting at the chamber's complex purpose. But what lay beyond left them in awe.

They ventured further into the chamber and were met with a genuinely astonishing sight: a starship unlike anything they had seen before. Its sleek design and advanced technology were alien and strangely familiar, sparking immediate speculation about its origin and capabilities. Amidst their amazement, the team couldn't help but wonder if this mysterious spacecraft was still operational after potentially millennia of dormancy. The implications of such a discovery were immense, suggesting the existence of advanced civilizations or technologies that could challenge their understanding of the Empire's history and place in the vastness of space.

As news of their incredible find spread, excitement grew among experts and enthusiasts alike. A new era of exploration and research was on the horizon, centered around this enigmatic craft at the heart of the chamber. Their upcoming investigations promised to unlock its secrets and spark widespread interest in their groundbreaking expedition.

As news of their incredible find spread, excitement grew among experts and enthusiasts alike. A new era of exploration and research was on the horizon, centered around this enigmatic spacecraft at the heart of the chamber. Their upcoming investigations promised to unlock its secrets and spark widespread interest in their groundbreaking expedition.

With this discovery, the future consumed all of Pope's thoughts. What would it mean for him and the Empire? Would this new knowledge be used for good or evil? The possibilities were endless, and Pope couldn't help but feel excitement and trepidation.

He began to plan, his mind racing with ideas of how this discovery could improve the Empire's standing in the world. Perhaps it could lead to new trade opportunities, alliances with other nations, or technological advances.

Pope knew he had to proceed with caution, but he couldn't ignore the potential this discovery held. So much was at stake, and the future was uncertain. But in that uncertainty, there was a glimmer of hope. Whatever the outcome, Pub was determined to make the most of this opportunity and shape the future of the Empire.

Stay tuned for the highly anticipated sequel to Survivor's Revenge: Survivor's Revenge II, which is coming soon.

Don't miss out!

Visit the website below and you can sign up to receive emails whenever Walter Keith publishes a new book. There's no charge and no obligation.

https://books2read.com/r/B-A-LSEMB-RNEQD

BOOKS2READ

Connecting independent readers to independent writers.